COMMANDER WILLIAM RIKER
FIRED THE IMPULSE
ENGINES . . .

. . . and the saucer section bucked like a bronco at the rodeo. Everyone, including Riker, was tossed to the deck, and the saucer shot straight up for several seconds. With a terrible groaning sound, the saucer stopped its ascent and hovered above the rain clouds, then it plunged into a monstrous belly dive.

The commander crawled back into his seat, hardly cognizant of the moaning and wounded people around him. He pulled back every flap and fired every thruster to try to bring them out of their nosedive, but he only succeeded in putting them into a deadly spiral.

Look for STAR TREK Fiction from Pocket Books

Star Trek: The Original Series

Star Trek: The Next Generation

Star Trek: Deep Space Nine

Star Trek: Voyager

STAR TREK
THE NEXT GENERATION®

ROGUE
SAUCER

JOHN VORNHOLT

POCKET BOOKS
New York   London   Toronto   Sydney   Tokyo   Singapore

An *Original* Publication of POCKET BOOKS

POCKET BOOKS, a division of Simon & Schuster Inc.
1230 Avenue of the Americas, New York, NY 10020

This book is published by Pocket Books, a division of
Simon & Schuster Inc., under exclusive license from
Paramount Pictures.

ISBN: 0-671-54917-0

First Pocket Books printing March 1996

10 9 8 7 6 5 4 3 2 1

POCKET and colophon are registered trademarks of
Simon & Schuster Inc.

Printed in the U.S.A.

For Mike and Denise Okuda, Rick Sternbach, and all the writers and editors responsible for those amazing STAR TREK reference books.

Thanks to Penny Peters, John Ordover, Lee Whiteside, John Wheeler, and Dan Duperre for their timely assistance.

HISTORIAN'S NOTE

This story takes place shortly after the events in *Preemptive Strike*.

ROGUE
SAUCER

Chapter One

"LONG-RANGE FREIGHTER, PAKLED SIGNATURE," said Lieutenant Commander Data. The android studied his readouts at the Ops console as his swift fingers brought up screen after screen. "They have tripped the primary and secondary buoys and are approaching the Demilitarized Zone at warp one."

Commander Will Riker rose from the command chair on the bridge of the *Enterprise* and took a stride forward. "Helm, lock in course to intercept, maximum warp."

"Yes, sir," replied Ensign Tate as her slim fingers plied the console. "Course laid in."

"Engage." Riker turned to glance at Lieutenant Worf at the tactical station. "Hail them and send an abstract of the Federation-Cardassian border agreement. Maybe they don't know they have to be searched before they can enter the DMZ."

"Yes, sir," answered the deep-voiced Klingon.

Data cocked his head. "It would be odd if a Pakled freighter had not heard of the border agreement. They are the most active traders in this sector." He added, "The freighter has increased speed."

"Increased speed?" Riker frowned. "Mr. Worf, did they understand our hail?"

The Klingon grumbled, "I believe they understood it all too well."

Riker stroked his bearded chin and smiled. "Just when I thought this was going to be a slow day. What is their ETA at the Demilitarized Zone?"

"Three point six minutes," answered Data.

Riker nodded. "Mr. Worf, ready a photon torpedo, match their course, and detonate it two hundred thousand kilometers in front of the Demilitarized Zone. Fire when ready. On screen."

Data punched up a long-range visual, as Worf solemnly reported, "Arming torpedo, targeting, torpedo away."

On the main viewer the torpedo was but a streak as it left the speeding ship and quickly attained a velocity several times greater than either the *Enterprise* or the Pakled freighter. In the distant starscape they saw a brilliant flash of light like a star going nova.

Worf smiled with satisfaction. "The Pakled freighter is coming out of warp."

Data adjusted the viewscreen to reveal a frog-shaped, khaki-colored freighter slowing to impulse power. It had clashing stripes of light blue and yellow on its boxy stern and was about the ugliest vessel Riker had ever seen.

"Hail them again." Riker tapped his comm badge and said, "Bridge to Captain Picard."

"Picard here," came a muffled voice.

"Sorry to interrupt your breakfast, sir, but we've just intercepted a Pakled freighter that was headed for the Demilitarized Zone. We'll scan for weapons in their cargo, but you should know that we had to fire a torpedo to get them to stop."

"Use caution," said the captain, "and keep me informed. Picard out."

Captain Picard dabbed a napkin to his lips and wiped it briefly under his patrician nose, then he pushed his chair back. Sitting across from him, Beverly Crusher gave him a concerned look. The attractive doctor looked a bit haggard this morning, and her normally full red hair was gathered loosely at the nape of her neck.

"Now, Jean-Luc," she whispered, "you're not going to leave a whole plate of Regulan eelbird eggs just sitting there. Guinan will be upset. She had to trade a case of Andolian brandy for those—they're too complex for the replicator."

"I don't see *you* eating anything," observed Picard.

The doctor shifted uneasily in her chair. "Well, I had a late dinner."

"Late dinner and late hours," said the captain disapprovingly. "In fact, I get the feeling you haven't slept in days, have you?"

Beverly smiled wanly. "Well, I'm three weeks

behind on the crew evaluations, I'm writing a paper on Derebian streptococci, and I'm directing a play. *Blood Wedding* by Lorca. One thing the evaluations are showing is that every member of this crew needs a shore leave."

Picard smiled briefly, then turned gloomy again. "I must admit, I'm not fond of our current assignment. Patrolling the Demilitarized Zone constantly reminds me that we are engaged in a war of attrition with our own people—Federation people."

Beverly shook her head sympathetically. "Jean-Luc, the Maquis aren't Federation anymore, they're renegades. When they chose to fight the Cardassians rather than obey the treaty, they became enemies of the Federation."

"I know," said the captain, his jaw tightening, "but I have a great deal of difficulty thinking of former comrades as enemies. In my fifty years of service, through war and peace, I don't believe anything more disheartening than this has happened. I abhor the whole idea of fighting former comrades and stopping ships that might be giving them aid and comfort."

Through the expansive window, Picard surveyed the star-studded blackness of space. "When I was a lad, I studied the writings of François, Duc de La Rochefoucauld. He said something that I have never fully understood until now. 'It is more shameful to distrust one's friends than to be deceived by them.'"

Beverly smiled wistfully, "Ah, Ro Laren?"

"That was the worst one," admitted Picard,

"because I delivered her into their hands." He pushed the plate of exotic poached eggs away from him. "Please tell Guinan that I'm sorry, but this matter with the freighter came up. If Riker has to board her, I should be on the bridge."

Suddenly a klaxon sounded, piercing the calm of the captain's quarters. "Red alert!" boomed Riker's voice over the comm system. "All command personnel to their stations!"

Picard bolted to his feet and glanced at Beverly, who jumped up and tapped her comm badge. "Crusher to sickbay!" she called.

The captain strode onto the bridge and was shocked to see Lieutenant Worf standing over his tactical console, spraying it with heat dampener. All around him sparks sputtered from various consoles, and acrid smoke drifted through the air.

"Report!"

Riker turned to face Picard. "Sir, after a debate, the Pakled freighter consented to lower her shields and let us scan her. We're trying to establish what happened next."

"Captain, I have a theory," said Data. "It would appear that they piggybacked a baryon particle beam onto our return sensor signal. It was a very sophisticated maneuver, requiring planning and a detailed knowledge of the *Enterprise's* bridge subsystems. Had they succeeded, they would have contaminated the bridge."

"Any damage to the rest of the ship?"

"No, sir," answered the android. "The damage was targeted at the main bridge and was restricted to the bridge by emergency containment fields. All command functions have been automatically routed to the battle bridge."

Picard frowned and looked at the main viewscreen, which was disconcertingly blank. "Where is the freighter now?"

"It is moving away from our port bow at a speed of Warp 2.1," the android replied. "This maneuver could not have been expected to disable the *Enterprise* for long, merely long enough to allow the freighter to escape. By now they have reached the Demilitarized Zone."

"Stand down from red alert," Picard ordered.

"I am sorry, Captain," said Data, "but we can issue no commands from the main bridge."

Picard scowled and tapped his communicator. "Picard to battle bridge."

"Crusher here," came the reply of the ship's doctor. *"Is it really as bad up there as my sensors indicate?"*

"Yes! You have command of the ship. Stand down from red alert." After a moment, the noise and flashing lights stopped, but Captain Picard still felt like a human red alert. He took a deep breath. "Thank you, Dr. Crusher. I see it was your turn in the rotation for the battle bridge."

"Wouldn't have missed it," she answered cheerfully.

"Picard out." The captain scowled at Riker. "As soon as we get back on our feet, I want to talk to a representative of the Pakled government."

"Sir, we can't be entirely certain they were Pakleds. Although the freighter had a Pakled signature, they returned our hail on audio only. Plus, I can't believe the Pakleds knew enough about our ship to do this to us."

Data added, "We can analyze their voice record."

"Make it so."

The android headed to the turbolift and stopped to look at the captain. "Sir, there appears to be no point in remaining on the bridge. It is nonfunctional."

Picard gazed at the mess that was his beloved bridge and heaved a sigh. "Right. Number One, you and Worf make sure that the bridge is secure, then join us in the battle bridge."

"Yes, sir." Riker took a deep breath and vowed, "This will never happen again."

"I should hope not." Picard lowered his head and bulled his way toward the turbolift.

An hour later the captain sat at the conference table in the observation lounge, surrounded by his senior officers: Dr. Crusher, Counselor Troi, Commander Riker, Lieutenant Commander Geordi La Forge, Lieutenant Commander Data, and Lieutenant Worf. It was time to hear suggestions and assess options.

"Engineering report," he said to La Forge.

The chief engineer sat forward in his chair and adjusted the VISOR that covered his eyes. "It doesn't look good. I've made an extensive list of the damage to the bridge, and you can access it on the computer. The bottom line is this—the baryon contamination of the bridge subsystems is too extensive for us to repair by ourselves. We have to put in to a starbase for repairs and a baryon sweep. As long as we're going to do that, we might as well update the entire bridge module. That will be my recommendation to Starfleet."

Picard felt a headache coming on behind his temporal lobe. "How long will that take?"

"Two or three days at best," said Geordi. "Then we'll need a few days of test flights. To be safe, we'd best count on a week. This is a major repair, but at least it's only to one section of the ship."

The captain nodded and turned to Data. "Did you analyze the voice records from that freighter?"

"Yes, sir," said the android. "The person who answered our hail from the freighter was not a Pakled—he was human. Considering our location, it is conceivable that the Maquis have either stolen or purchased a Pakled freighter for the purpose of running arms into the Demilitarized Zone. In addition, they obviously have someone with intimate knowledge of the *Enterprise*'s bridge subsystems and scanning procedures."

Riker spoke for everyone, "Ro."

Data nodded. "That is my supposition. Lieutenant Ro recently received advanced tactical training from Starfleet, and that may have included the use of baryon particle beams for the purpose of sabotage."

Worf pounded his fist on the table. "We still have warp drive and all our weapons—let us go after them!"

Picard held up his hand in warning. "If the

Enterprise entered the Demilitarized Zone, it could start a war with the Cardassians. We have to accept that fact that we were bested in this confrontation. That's the trouble with fighting the Maquis—they have dozens of former Starfleet officers, and they know us better than we know ourselves."

Picard ran his hand over his smooth crown. "It seems we have no alternative but to put in to a starbase for repairs."

"Plus rest and relaxation," said Beverly Crusher. "Everyone on this ship needs a shore leave, so I'm not disappointed that we have to dock at a starbase for a week. Let's pick a base with some decent recreational facilities—like Starbase 211. It's fairly close, and they have three permanent museums, including the Kraybon Collection of archeological artifacts."

That suggestion brought a fleeting smile to Picard's face. "Ah, yes, I could lose myself quite easily for a week in the Kraybon Collection. I can certainly check to see if Starbase 211 has adequate repair facilities. I must admit, a week off from border patrol doesn't sound too dreadful. Are there any other suggestions?"

Data nodded. "I will write a new subroutine to check returning scan signals for baryon beams."

"Make it so," said the captain. "I'd better get started on my report to Starfleet. I'll ask about shore leave. Anything else?"

Worf gritted his teeth. "What are we going to do about Ro Laren?"

The captain shook his head. "Mr. Worf, we don't

know for certain that she was involved. There are many Maquis with knowledge of Galaxy-class vessels."

Picard shook off the disturbing thought of Ro Laren sabotaging her own—her former—ship, but she had chosen her own destiny, and in a way, he had helped shape that destiny. The captain rose to his feet and said curtly, "Dismissed."

Timothy Wiley, a handsome young human with a bristling red mustache, stepped upon the transporter platform of the *Shufola* and looked at the elder Bajoran at the transporter console. He could see Vylor struggling with the outmoded trim-pot controls, trying to stabilize the settings at a safe level for humans.

Wiley forced himself to the center of the glowing disc, which was humming disconcertingly. He smiled wanly. "You're sure you're not going to turn me into Hungarian goulash?"

"I don't know what that is," answered Vylor, "but you will either be on the planet in a few moments, or you'll be in the hands of the Prophets."

The young man cleared his throat. "Do the Prophets like humans?"

"Of course. The Emissary is a human." Vylor peered at his instruments and shrugged. "This is as accurate as it's going to get. No wonder the Pakleds sold us this craft so cheaply. I still wish there was some other way."

Wiley shook his head. "We can't risk breaking radio silence, and I must *see* the Architect. Besides, we've already gotten our money's worth out of this freighter, even if I don't come back."

"We will return for you tomorrow at the appointed time," the white-haired Bajoran assured him. "Give my best to the Architect."

"I will, and you keep working on that tractor beam. We need to be able to tow a ship at warp speeds."

"It's almost ready."

Wiley squared his shoulders and took a deep breath. "Energize."

Then he screwed his eyes shut, not anxious to meet the Prophets, Saint Peter, or whoever greeted those unlucky enough to be using an old Pakled transporter. He felt a stinging along his skin that was much more intense than the polite tingling that accompanied a Federation transporter. With huge relief, he felt shifting rubble under his feet and smelled an obnoxious odor redolent of burning rubber. Then he opened his eyes upon a scene that was worthy of Dante's *Inferno,* and he wondered briefly whether he had gone by mistake to the home of lost souls.

It was night on this part of New Hope, in a ruined city that had been burning nonstop for years, ever since the final Cardassian attack before the first treaty took effect. The black buildings, or what was left of them, were constructed from a pitchlike substance extracted from the swamps and trees that covered most of New Hope. The pitch was naturally flame-resistant, except when subjected to thermoactive weapons, which was exactly what the Cardassians had used on the city. Now the black towers and spires that had once housed half a million people burned in perpetuity—a dead city of smoldering torches rising hundreds of meters into the sky. It reminded Timothy Wiley of the smokestack cities of twentieth-century Earth that he had seen in old video logs.

He coughed, momentarily overcome by the dreadful fumes, and staggered off the rubble. The young man patted the small pouch strapped to his waist to make sure that he still had his precious cargo, then he stopped to get his bearings. A charred, grinning skeleton lay on the ground a few meters away, its right hand outstretched in what looked like a haphazard manner. Wiley knew it was not haphazard at all, and he carefully picked his way through the debris in the direction the dead man was pointing.

Flames licking the sky provided plenty of light, and he had no problem finding the next signpost— a decrepit subway entrance. Once made of gleaming metal, the entrance and stairs had melted into a grotesque crater with crude symbols painted all over it. Wiley spotted the painted heart with an arrow through it, and he turned in the direction of the arrow. By now, he was skirting perilously close to a burning building, and he could feel the intense heat from the fire prickling his skin, then drenching him with sweat. The ground was littered with pebbles of melted glass that crunched under his feet.

Finally, he saw an old electric car that was also little more than a misshapen lump of metal. But the door hung on its hinges, still functional. He opened the door as he had been instructed, squeezed inside, and sat on the threadbare seat of the vehicle. Musty smells were almost overpowering, and Wiley held his breath as he pushed the panel that once turned on the lights. Immediately, the seat began to lower into the ground, and another seat slid into place above him.

There were more musty smells but little to see in the tube that brought him several stories beneath the planet's surface. He finally stopped, and a metal door opened at his side. Wiley stepped out to see an armed woman who was wearing a cold-weather mask and holding a phaser rifle.

"Name?" asked the woman.

"Blue Moon," answered Timothy Wiley.

The woman nodded and finally smiled. "You were successful?"

"Yes." Wiley grinned and patted the pouch on his hip.

"Good. Architect is waiting to see you." The woman stepped aside and motioned him down a narrow corridor.

Wiley walked quickly, because he was very anxious to meet the Architect, a new addition from Starfleet who had enormous knowledge of Starfleet procedures. In a short time, she had revolutionized the random operations of dozens of disconnected cells, making the Maquis' forays bolder and more successful. This latest triumph was a good example of her genius, and so was the fact that she had turned a devastated planet into her command post. New Hope was surely the last place the Cardassian death squads would look for a Maquis cell.

Weapons smuggling was only the beginning. They had plans, much bigger plans.

At the end of the corridor, Wiley found a simple wooden door, and he pushed it open to enter a cramped office full of computer equipment and sensors. A slim woman with short-cropped dark hair was hunched over a terminal, entering data. She turned to face him, and he was surprised to see that she wasn't wearing a mask to hide her identity. Furthermore, the notches on the bridge of her nose revealed her to be a Bajoran. He hadn't realized that a Bajoran could rise that far in Starfleet.

He also noticed that she was very attractive in an intense sort of way.

"Architect?" he asked.

She nodded curtly. "You made it through?"

He grinned and smoothed back his mustache with pride. "We certainly did. The baryon particles on the return scan worked exactly as you said they would. Not only did we get through, the ship we crippled was none other than the *Enterprise!*"

She lowered her chin, and he could see unmistakable sadness in her lovely brown eyes. "Were there casualties?"

"None on our part, but we didn't stick around long enough to find out if *they* had any. At least now we know we can get through the blockade."

Architect shook her head glumly. "No, we can never use that trick again. The crew of the *Enterprise* is the best there is. They undoubtedly know exactly what we did, and every ship in Starfleet will be prepared for it next time. It was unfortunate that you met the *Enterprise*—I was hoping you'd run up against a small cruiser full of ensigns fresh out of the Academy."

She stood up and held out her hand. "Do you have a sample?"

"Yes!" He opened up his pouch and took out a Klingon disruptor pistol, which he dropped into her palm. She studied the sleek weapon with its molded grip and phase-disruption chambers.

"No 'stun' settings on this baby," said Wiley. "Armed with these disruptors, we can go up against Cardassians, Starfleet . . ."

"No!" she said sharply. "These weapons are never to be used against Starfleet. The Federation is not our enemy."

"Well, they sure as hell aren't our friends," countered Wiley, taken aback by her attitude. "They *did* fire at us."

The slim Bajoran narrowed her eyes at him. "If the *Enterprise* had fired at you, you wouldn't be here."

"Well," he admitted, "they fired past us in order to get us to stop."

"Standard procedure," she said. "What about the rest of our plan? Is Peacock in place?"

"Yes. I got the word before we left Klingon space. Peacock has gotten his new assignment and is right where he's supposed to be, just waiting for the proper set of circumstances. The *Shufola* will make her deliveries and come back to get me tomorrow. Then we're on our way to bring back the Big Prize!" Wiley grinned with anticipation.

To his surprise, Architect glared at him. "Remember one thing—no Starfleet personnel are to be injured on this mission. The Maquis spent a long time setting up this plan, and it was designed to go without a hitch and without a single casualty. I want your word on this—you won't hurt any Starfleet personnel."

Wiley lifted his hands helplessly. "I'll try. But I don't know why you're so concerned about the Federation. They deserted *us.*"

"They're still part of us, and we're still part of them. They thought they were buying peace by drawing up new boundaries, but you can't buy peace from creatures like the Cardassians. They made a terrible mistake, and we have to prove it to them. The long-range plan is to drive the Cardassians out, return people to their homes, and rejoin the Federation. Never lose sight of that."

"Okay," said Wiley. "I guess someday you want to go back to Starfleet, huh."

The young Bajoran shook her head sadly. "It's too late for that, too late for me. Starfleet doesn't know most of the members of the Maquis, but they know their former officers. There's no going back for me. In fact, sometimes I wonder if I'll ever leave this planet alive."

Wiley felt a pang in his heart for this beautiful young woman. He wanted to wrap her in his arms and assure her that there would be a happy ending to their trials, but he didn't know if that was truly the case. Before joining the Maquis, Wiley had been a navigator on commercial freighters, and Starfleet hardly knew he was alive. He could conceivably go back to his former career when this was all over, with Starfleet none the wiser; but it was different for the Architect. She must have been a highly trusted officer to have learned all she knew about Starfleet, he realized, and she had given it all up for a bunch of displaced colonists.

He started to reach for her, and she drew back. With a hoarse voice, she said, "Go now. My assistant will get you something to eat and find you a place to sleep. You have done very well and have brought us closer to our goals."

With that summary dismissal, she sat at her desk and again hunched over her instruments. When she continued to ignore him, Timothy Wiley pushed open the door and walked out. He glanced back at the young woman, thinking he would never be as alone as she was.

Chapter Two

CAPTAIN PICARD WAS BEAMING as he shoved the
computer padd under Beverly Crusher's nose.
"Look at this," he said excitedly, "the Kraybon
Collection contains the only known example of a
Fire Scepter from the ruins of Iconia Primus. It's
nonfunctional, of course, but it's still a remarkable
artifact. The Demons, as they called themselves,
could supposedly travel between planets without
the need for spacecraft."

Beverly smiled agreeably. "I remember the leg-
ends quite well, Jean-Luc." A server passed their
table in the Ten-Forward lounge, and Beverly held
out her cup. "Could I please have some more
decaffeinated cocoa?"

18

"Certainly," said the young man, taking her cup and rushing off.

"Decaffeinated cocoa?" asked Picard. "I should think you would want something more . . . more stimulating. We're going on shore leave . . . though I can hardly imagine it."

"I can," said the doctor, "but I intend to sleep for about the first twenty-four hours. After that, I'll be happy to tour the Kraybon Collection with you, although I'm personally more interested in the traveling exhibit from the Hermitage Museum. Twentieth-century Impressionists, that's more my idea of a good time."

"Absolutely!" agreed Picard, taking her hands in his. "Beverly, coming here was an excellent idea. Not only do they have a first-class repair facility, but the prospect of all these museums is marvelous."

She gazed back at him with velvety green eyes. "I haven't seen you so happy in a long time. Maybe we should get our bridge blown up more often."

The captain looked pained. "I think that's a rather drastic way to get shore leave, but it did seem to work. I just hope nobody is going to send me a bill."

Their young server appeared with Beverly's refill of cocoa, and Picard released Beverly's hands. "Is there anything else?" asked the server. "We're shutting down in a few minutes to prepare to disembark."

"No, we're fine," the captain answered cheerfully. "What are you going to do on your shore leave, Bartlett?"

"I'm catching a transport to Tau Ceti III," said the young man. "I haven't seen my parents in two years, and I don't know when I'll get another leave."

Picard nodded approvingly. "Very commendable."

Bartlett frowned for a moment. "Do you really think the repairs will take a week?"

"That is Commander La Forge's best estimate, and he's seldom wrong about such things."

"By the way," said Beverly, looking around the tasteful saloon, "where is Guinan?"

Bartlett smiled. "She's still packing. Can't decide which hats to bring."

Picard chuckled and waved the young man off. "Don't let us delay you. Enjoy yourself."

"Thank you, sir."

The captain glanced out the nearest window, and his smile got even wider as he saw Starbase 211 looming into view. It resembled a vast DNA model lit up with Christmas tree lights. Virtually everything the Federation had to offer its space-faring members was available at 211, from a thriving artistic community to a repair facility that was second to none. Its relative proximity to Cardassian-controlled space gave 211 a considerable Starfleet presence. As they drew closer to the spidery city in space, he could see starships hanging from its appendages like flies caught in a glimmering web.

Picard's comm badge chirped, and a familiar voice said, "Battle bridge to Captain Picard."

He tapped it and answered, "Yes, Number One."

"Captain, we have been cleared to proceed to docking bay 27. We anticipate opening the airlocks in three minutes."

"Take her in, Number One."

"Yes, sir," said Riker cheerfully. "Enjoy your leave, sir. Bridge out."

The captain beamed at Beverly. "Shall we be going?"

She smiled back and picked up her valise. "Lead on."

Picard grabbed his small duffel bag and followed the crowd out of Ten-Forward. A line was forming at the extendable docking port on the underbelly of the saucer section, but they made way for Dr. Crusher and Captain Picard. The captain nodded appreciatively as he took his place at the front of the line. Rank did have its privileges, and he was not above exercising them, on occasion.

The captain thought about his plans for the day. After checking into his quarters on the station, he would meet with Captain Slarn, the base commander, then meet with La Forge and the repair crew. With any luck at all, these meetings would be perfunctory and he would be left to explore the wonders of the Kraybon Collection all afternoon. Then to meet with Beverly for dinner, perhaps catch a play or a concert, a late night *aperitif.* . . .

The captain's mind was wandering when Will Riker's voice boomed over the ship. "All hands, prepare to dock!"

After a gentle and reassuring *ker-chunk,* the ship came to rest against the dock. Security officers took up position around the airlocks, and a young ensign saluted Picard off the ship. As they made their way down the ramp, the captain and the doctor chatted pleasantly about restaurants on the cosmopolitan space station. They entered a vast terminal and craned their necks to take in the entire geodesic ceiling, which had to be at least a hundred meters high. Stars shimmered beyond the ceiling, and meteors streaked across the dome in alarmingly close proximity. It was a moment later, when a ringed planet swept across the blackness, that Picard realized he was looking at a simulation, not the actual starscape surrounding them. As he recalled, the walls of the dome were actually tri-polymer alloys several meters thick.

Despite its immense size, the terminal was bustling, and Jean-Luc and Beverly were swallowed up in a sea of humanoid and alien creatures. *That was almost the best part of shore leave,* thought the captain, *the feeling of being just one of the crowd.* He could feel the weight of responsibility slipping off his shoulders to be replaced by a feeling of lightness and anticipation. The Fire Scepter—he was tempted to pull rank again and try to be allowed to handle it. Yes, thought the captain, he would be making very good friends among the curators of the various museums on Starbase 211.

"Captain Picard!" said a sharp female voice.

Picard froze. His shoulders caved downward, and his stomach knotted. Tight-lipped, he whispered to Beverly, "I'm about to get the bill."

He whirled around and was met by a stern scowl from a severe-looking woman with sandy-colored hair, wearing the pips of an admiral. His smile began to melt. Picard could face Borg, Romulans, Q, Cardassians, even Worf's relatives, but Vice Admiral Alynna Nechayev was the only force in the universe that chilled him to the marrow.

"Admiral Nechayev!" said Beverly with all the charm she could muster. "What a pleasant surprise. What a coincidence that you're here on 211."

"It's no coincidence," said the admiral with a steely edge to her voice. "Now, if you will excuse us, Dr. Crusher, I must speak privately with the captain."

"But our plans . . ." Beverly swallowed her words and came to attention. "Yes, Admiral Nechayev. It was a pleasure seeing you again."

She hurried off, which was exactly what Picard would have done had he been given the opportunity. Like a brave French aristocrat on his way to the *guillotine*, he turned to Admiral Nechayev and jutted out his jaw. "I am at your disposal."

"Thank you, Captain. We have several important matters to discuss." She tapped her communicator. "Energize."

Their bodies sparkled into columns of light and rematerialized in a conference room with a view of what appeared to be a maze of handball courts stretching into the distance. On closer inspection, Picard could see several matches in progress, and he envied the way the players were shedding their cares by the act of sheer physical exertion. His cares, on the other hand, were mounting by the moment.

"We won't be overheard here." Nechayev pressed a panel on the wall, and the windows turned opaque. Picard sighed and looked back at the diminutive admiral.

"I have read your report about the incident at the border," said Nechayev, shaking her head. "I still cannot understand how the flagship of the fleet can allow an ancient Pakled freighter to escape, *plus* sustain enough damage to bring itself to spacedock."

The captain could feel his Adam's apple drying out, still he answered, "As I indicated in my report, my crew followed standard procedures, not expecting a Pakled freighter to have detailed knowledge of our bridge subsystems. Commander Data has already written a subroutine that will check for baryon particle beams on returning sensor signals."

Nechayev regarded him severely. "You weren't even on the bridge, Captain. No matter how you cut it, the handling of the freighter was very slipshod."

That was the moment when Picard decided to spell it out for his superior. "With all due respect, Admiral, we cannot be expected to go up against former Starfleet officers without risking some losses. They know our vessels, our equipment, our personnel, and our weaknesses. Our standard procedures are ineffective or downright dangerous when used against them. The Maquis have good leadership, good intelligence, and are highly motivated. Plus, they have a hiding place where we can't chase after them!"

Admiral Nechayev took a deep breath, and Picard braced himself to be chewed out again. Instead, the middle-aged woman balled her hands into fists and paced the length of the conference room. "Captain, I have warned Starfleet many times about the problems of containing the Maquis. I come from a country that has a history of terrible civil wars, and nothing is more dangerous than a revolution from within. When a substantial number of citizens begin to suspect their own government is incompetent . . . it is the beginning of the end."

Then she turned and pointed her finger at him. "However, it is not our job to question the political decisions of the Federation. We have peace with Cardassia, and the price of that peace is the Maquis, which is *our* responsibility. It's up to us to put them out of business, no matter how difficult the circumstances, no matter *who* they are."

"Understood," said Picard, bristling at the implications of her speech.

Admiral Nechayev narrowed her pale eyes at him. "Ro was *your* responsibility, Captain," she reminded him. "You were her contact on the mission."

Slowly Picard answered, "That is true—I was her contact—and no one feels the loss of Ro Laren more acutely than I. However, I would remind you that mine was not the only opinion involved in picking her for the mission. We both agreed it was a gamble that was worth taking, even if it backfired on us."

Nechayev nodded somberly and stared down at

the glossy conference table. "Yes, we share responsibility on Ro Laren, and you can be sure that I've caught it from above. That is why you haven't been reprimanded, Captain, because I took full responsibility for the defection of Lieutenant Ro."

"I'm sure we'll get a chance to redeem ourselves," said Picard, trying to sound upbeat.

The admiral smiled slightly and gazed at him with her hazel eyes. "Funny you should say that, Captain. The opportunity to redeem ourselves has already presented itself, as a direct result of the damage to your bridge. When was the last time you performed an emergency saucer separation?"

Picard cleared his throat apprehensively. "It has been some time, Admiral."

"Yes, I know. I can think of numerous instances where you have faced sufficient danger to warrant saucer separation, but you always seem to resist. Some might say you have willfully risked the lives of nonessential personnel and families."

The captain stiffened and said, "Every person stationed aboard the *Enterprise* has chosen to be there, and they are aware of the risks we face. As for saucer separation, I have considered it on many occassions, but the problem is that the saucer section itself doesn't have warp drive. In most instances, it can't run far enough or fast enough to escape the danger. I will admit, I prefer to keep my ship whole, but I wouldn't hesitate to separate the saucer if I thought it would really save lives."

In a conciliatory tone, he added, "On our trip here, we had to operate from the battle bridge, and

I have considerable respect for that oft-neglected part of the ship. Still, it's not the *real* bridge."

Nechayev looked at him with satisfaction. "Yes, you and the *Enterprise* are a perfect choice for this mission." She leaned across the table and gazed at him. "You talk about the saucer section and its inability to escape from danger, but you know it has one unique feature—it can survive reentry through a planetary atmosphere, and then crash-land."

"Theoretically," said Picard. "I certainly would never want to try it."

"You're right," agreed Nechayev. "We've never been able to test the procedure."

Picard was beginning to warm to this topic, glad not to be discussing the Maquis or Ro Laren anymore. "I can scarcely imagine how desperate the situation would be to risk crash-landing the saucer section on a strange planet. In most scenarios we're talking about the hull section already being destroyed or with a warp-core breech imminent. Life-support systems on the saucer are probably failing. Every computer model we've done shows that the saucer would survive, yes, but it would be reduced to a pile of junk. What if it happened on a planet with emerging technology? Finding the wreckage could destroy their entire culture."

"All good points," conceded Admiral Nechayev, "but *our* computer models show that a saucer section is likely to need the ability to crash-land on a planet someday. It's going to be more likely as we get more Galaxy-class ships in the fleet. You know, Captain, not all officers are as reticent about saucer separation as you are."

"I would do it without hesitation if the circumstances warranted it," Picard repeated.

"I'm glad to hear you say that, Captain." Admiral Nechayev leaned across the table and stared at him with cold, hazel eyes. "You wanted a chance to redeem yourself? Starfleet is not pleased by the fact that emergency-landing a saucer section badly damages it in every scenario we've tested. So we've built a prototype saucer section with improved forcefields and dampening fields, in the hope that it can survive atmospheric reentry, land, *and* be relaunched.

"The prototype has special thrusters that can lift it into the atmosphere, where a tractor beam from an orbiting ship can pull it into orbit. Theoretically, the hull section could resurrect its own saucer section from the planet's surface. If this proves successful, we won't risk leaving all that valuable technology behind for indigenous people to dig up."

Picard could feel his jaw hanging open. "You're going to *test* this?"

"No," said Nechayev with a glint in her eye, *"you're* going to test it."

The captain could feel himself starting to sputter, but luckily Admiral Nechayev didn't give him time to respond. "You have exactly what we need for this mission—an experienced crew and a Galaxy-class hull section that isn't busy doing anything else. The prototype saucer section is en route and will arrive in six hours. That will give you just enough time to assemble a skeleton crew."

"One moment," said Picard, barely containing his anger, "permission to speak freely, Admiral."

"Very well."

"Admiral, this is an extremely dangerous mission you're talking about, and my crew has been promised shore leave. Quite frankly, I'm not sure you could land a Galaxy-class saucer section and walk away from it, let alone expect the thing to *fly* again. I can't imagine who in their right mind would think up such a scheme."

Admiral Nechayev glared at him and seemed to be chewing on the inside of her cheeks. *"I* thought it up, Captain Picard, along with my new aide. Your negligence brought the *Enterprise* into Starbase 211 with a damaged saucer section, and I intend to use her hull section for this test, whether you like it or not. If you do not wish to command the mission, I will find somebody else."

"No, no," said Picard quickly, remembering the last time Nechayev turned his ship over to another captain. It had been a disaster, especially for the morale of his crew. He didn't even want to see *half* of his ship turned over to somebody else.

"I would like to make this a volunteer mission," he said finally. "I believe the danger warrants such consideration."

Nechayev softened her stern expression a shade. "I have no objection to that, Captain. I believe we need only about fifteen people, and I agree with your doctor's report that your crew needs this shore leave. I want the vast majority of them to continue their leave as planned. You have my permission to exclude crew members with families or anyone you wish to see continue their shore leave."

"Thank you," said Picard, realizing that his own shore leave and exploration of the Kraybon Collection would have to be postponed indefinitely.

Admiral Nechayev consulted her timepiece. "Have your crew at docking bay twenty-seven at 1600 hours."

With that, the slight admiral strode to the door, waited for it to open, and started out. She stopped just long enough to look back at him. "Oh, one more thing. To make the emergency saucer separation as real as possible, an alien attack and a red alert will be simulated. My aide is doing the programming."

Picard felt like rolling his eyes toward heaven, but he managed to keep a benign expression on his face until Admiral Nechayev dashed off. He slumped into one of the conference chairs and dropped his duffel bag onto the floor. His hand felt stiff, and he glanced at it to see the imprint of the bag handle still fresh on his palm.

The captain pushed a panel on the table and took one more longing look at the people playing handball in a maze of clean, white courts.

Will Riker smiled at the young Deltan woman as she coyly brushed her ear feathers against her bald head. She was delicate yet shapely, and her skin was like alabaster, an impression only fortified by the lack of hair on her head and, he assumed, her entire body. She more than made up for the lack of natural adornment with an array of lavender feathers grafted to her ears and along the sides of her slim neck.

"They said the transport to Omicron IV was due today," she told him. "I'd like to stay, but I've done my fieldwork and have to go back to class. You know how it is,"

"I know," said Riker, leaning forward with his chin resting in the palm of his hand. He gazed into lavender eyes that matched her feathers. "But I happen to know that graduate study in terraforming is a self-paced program. Taking a few extra days to get home wouldn't make any difference."

He sighed wistfully. "I can tell you, it would make a great deal of difference to a lonely man who has been in space for many months without a leave."

She tilted her perfectly oval face. "Are you telling me, Commander Riker, that there are no women aboard the *Enterprise?*"

"None as beautiful as you," he said. "Besides, who has time for women when there's a galaxy to explore? Not to mention clashes with Borg, Romulans, and other dangerous foes. Every time we leave dock, I frankly don't know if I'll ever see another starbase again, or if I'll ever have another leave. Are you sure you can't take just a day or two to show me around? This may be my last time."

She ran her delicate finger around the lip of her glass. "I suppose another day or two won't make any difference."

The commander grinned. "That's the spirit!

You'll go a long way toward making this the most memorable shore leave I've ever had."

"Where do you want to start?"

Riker resisted the first answer that popped into his head. "To be honest with you," he said innocently, "I haven't even found my quarters yet. Perhaps we could just take a stroll in that general direction. If you see something you'd like to point out, please do so."

"I'm ready to go," replied the Deltan, batting her nude eyelids. "But I should pay my bill."

Riker looked around the bistro, with its checkered tablecloths and holographic candles that looked like open flames in wine bottles, and he couldn't see a server anywhere. If he didn't find someone to pay soon, he would take his escort's slender arm and bolt from the place, coming back later to pay. Just then, an old Ferengi carrying a tray shuffled past, and Riker waved to him, knowing you could always get a Ferengi to take your money.

"They scanned me when I came in," said Riker. "Can I put the lady's bill on my account?"

"Certainly," lisped the toothless old Ferengi, looking like an elephant as he bowed. He showed Riker the amount, but the commander barely glanced at the padd as he took the stylus and signed the screen. His eyes were for the enchanting creature sitting across from him.

"Shall we?" he asked, rising to his feet. He pulled out the young Deltan's chair and helped her to her feet, drawing a sharp breath when he saw how tall she was. Despite her delicate, hairless features, she was an Amazon dressed in a form-hugging tube dress.

That was when his comm badge sounded. He stared accusingly at the noisy badge. "Don't they know I'm on leave?"

"Apparently not," answered the Deltan with a deadpan expression.

He tapped his badge. "Riker here."

"This is Captain Picard," came a stern voice. "Sorry to bother you, Number One, but I have to talk to you immediately."

Riker smiled uncomfortably and lowered his voice. "Excuse me, sir, but could we do this at another time?"

"I'm afraid not. I'm in conference room six, deck four of the fitness center. If you have any problem finding it, you can beam directly here, by authorization of Admiral Nechayev."

"Admiral Nechayev," said Riker, taking a dry swallow.

He heard an impatient sigh, and he turned to see the statuesque Deltan stalk away. He was tempted to follow, but the captain's voice broke in to his thoughts.

"On the double, Number One."

"Yes, sir. Riker out."

The old Ferengi server chuckled and stroked his dangling earlobes. "Ah, great pheromones. Those Deltan women are very possessive, always want to be first in your life. But if you get one to love you— oh, my, are you in for a treat."

"Shut up," muttered Riker.

Chapter Three

GEORDI LA FORGE took the madras porkpie hat and set it at a rakish angle on Data's head. "Now you're ready to play some pool."

"I do not see how wearing a hat makes me any more ready to play billiards," responded the android.

"Pool," Geordi corrected him. "They're two different games."

"I was speaking of the larger historical category," said Data, "of which pool is a variation."

"You need sunglasses, too," suggested Geordi, putting a pair of dark, jazzy shades over Data's yellow eyes. "Now you're ready to play pool."

Data had the price of the hat and sunglasses put on his account, and they left the shop to stroll along

Starbase 211's main mall, quaintly named The Milky Way. They were headed back to a pool parlor they had passed several doors down, next to a bookstore selling holonovels.

"I believe the amount I paid for the hat and sunglasses is exorbitant," complained Data.

Geordi laughed. *"Now* you decide that. Come on, Data, we're on shore leave! Being foolish with money is traditional when you're on leave."

The android stood steadfast. "Spending money foolishly is not a vice I wish to cultivate."

"Okay," conceded Geordi, "but I can't see you retiring to a beach house on Pacifica, so what are you going to spend your money on?"

The android straightened his hat. "Perhaps a present for Spot. She seemed displeased about being left in a kennel."

"You can visit her every day while we're on leave."

"Yes," said Data, "but if we were still aboard the *Enterprise,* I could share habitation with my cat as always. I confess, I do not understand the appeal of shore leave, which only serves to interrupt everyone's routine."

"That's exactly the point," said Geordi with frustration. "We do different things, sleep different places, see different people, and when we go back to our routine we feel better about it."

"Is there any scientific data for this phenomenon, or is it all anecdotal?"

Geordi laughed and shook his head. "We're here."

They stopped outside a storefront that had

opaque windows through which normal vision could not penetrate. That didn't bother Geordi— the infrared sensors in his VISOR could see the coolness of the pool tables amidst the heat of living beings, bustling about, bending over. He smiled.

"Looks like there are women inside. Try to enjoy yourself, okay?"

As if in response, the android's comm badge beeped. "Data," he answered.

"This is the captain. I need to talk to you immediately about a volunteer mission. I'm in conference room six, deck four of the fitness center."

"Yes, sir," answered Data. "Commander La Forge is with me. Do you require his presence?"

After a moment, Picard answered, "I was hoping to give Mr. La Forge his full shore leave, but I should give him a choice. So yes, I would like both of you to report. Picard out."

Lieutenant Worf watched the Andorian fakir with mounting interest, wondering if he was truly going to lie down on a bed of laser styluses. In addition to the bed of styluses, there was a box of crystallized pumice; the gleaming shards looked impressive, but Worf suspected that the fragments had been worn into pebbles with hardly a sharp edge left among them. The styluses, however, were a different matter; they pulsated in unison, waiting to etch their way through alloys, polymers, or flesh. The Klingon nodded grimly at the notion of sub- jecting a person's backside to an array of etching tools. If the Andorian's religion demanded such suffering, it must forge a spirit of great nobility, Worf concluded approvingly.

The gawky, blue-skinned fakir was dressed in a simple loincloth, and he talked to his audience in a dull monotone, all the time bowing respectfully. The audience consisted of about twenty people gathered in the courtyard outside the entrance to the Osstan Terrarium. Worf's original destination had been the terrarium, which housed a collection of reptiles from all over the galaxy, exhibited in natural settings. If he was lucky, he might witness the feeding of a Tangolese Hechid, which was very rare in captivity.

"Get on with it," Worf found himself muttering.

"Yes, get on with it!" shouted a small Saurian to his left. The alien craned his long neck at Worf and snapped his beak in what might have been a smile.

"Let him do his presentation," said a familiar voice with a lilting accent. Worf whirled around to see Deanna Troi, wearing a blue, strapless evening gown. Waves of dark hair fell over her shoulders.

"Hello, Deanna," he said. "You look very impressive."

She stepped close enough to whisper, "Thank you, Worf. I'm going to a concert in an hour. What are you doing besides harassing this poor man, who is only trying to explain his religion?"

Worf cleared his throat with embarrassment. "I did not mean to sound impatient."

Deanna smiled. "He's only doing the stunts so you'll listen to his spiel. Anyway, he's about to begin."

Worf turned to see the Andorian walk slowly

toward the box of crystallized pumice. He lowered his head, as if aiming his blue antennae at some invisible force within the glimmering shards. Then he stepped into the box with his bare feet and began walking upon the pumice. There were a few appreciative gasps from the audience, but Worf was unimpressed—he understood that this trick was just the warm-up for the bed of styluses.

"What are you doing after you watch this?" asked Deanna, who gripped his attention much more effectively than the fakir.

"I intended to see the feeding of the Tangolese Hechid," he explained. "The Hechid itself is a sluggish lizard, but it has a symbiotic creature, the Machud, living in its mouth. The Machud casts a membranelike net upon their mutual prey—to witness a pair of these creatures feeding is to witness admirable teamwork."

Deanna managed a polite smile. "I see. If you're determined to watch lizards feed, I don't suppose you'd be interested in hearing a Bynar octet."

"A Bynar octet?" asked the Klingon hesitantly. Atonal music with endless repetitions was not exactly his idea of stimulating entertainment. Often he felt like giving in to his growing attraction for Deanna Troi, but just as often the differences between them became all too apparent.

Before he could answer, Worf heard scattered applause and turned to see the Andorian exit from the box of pumice. Looking grave, he walked slowly to the bed of laser styluses and stopped to gaze at the pulsating needles. As the Andorian began to lower himself upon the bed, the Klingon could feel Deanna Troi move closer and grip his arm. Their attention was riveted upon the fakir as his blue skin came in contact with the glowing styluses.

Then Worf's comm badge beeped. With a scowl, he took a few steps away from the crowd and answered, "Worf here."

"Picard. I'm sorry to interrupt your shore leave, Lieutenant, but there's an important matter to discuss." He gave him directions to the conference room that overlooked the fitness center. "On the double."

"Yes, sir," answered Worf. He tapped his comm badge to end the transmission and saw Deanna looking curiously at him.

"What was that about?"

"I do not know. The captain needs to see me immediately. It seems that my shore leave may be over." He bowed stiffly to the Betazoid and stole a glance over the heads of the crowd. "Another time?"

"Another time," she answered thoughtfully.

"I tell you, there's something going on, and we're being kept in the dark." Deanna Troi put her hands on her slim hips, which were accentuated by the slinky evening gown. From her attitude it was clear that she wanted to know what Beverly Crusher was going to do about this conspiracy.

The doctor sighed and hung her own black evening gown back in the closet. She had a feeling she wasn't going to get to wear the lovely dress, and even if she wore it, there wouldn't be anyone around to appreciate it.

"How do you know we're being kept in the dark?" she asked Deanna.

"I asked the base computer for several people's whereabouts. The captain, Will, Worf, Geordi, Data—they're all in conference room six at the fitness center. You were the only one in her quarters."

The doctor decided to tackle the obvious explanation first. "If they're all in the fitness center, could they be playing a game or working out?"

"I don't think so. I sensed stress in the captain's voice."

That reminded Beverly of something. "There is another possibility. Vice Admiral Nechayev is on the base, and the last I saw of Captain Picard, he was with her. This could have something to do with the admiral."

Deanna shrugged and looked down at her elegant gown. "Well, I'm not exactly dressed for a visit to the fitness center, but I would like to see it. Want to come along?"

"Sure," agreed Beverly. "I could use a massage."

With her unwavering sense of direction, Deanna Troi led Dr. Crusher through the sprawling starbase, taking a series of turbolifts that carried them up, down, sideways, and diagonally. In less than three minutes, they arrived at the fitness center and found the conference rooms on deck four.

Beverly glanced over the railing at the neat rows

of white courts below them. "I wouldn't mind a racquetball game either."

"Some other time," replied Deanna. The counselor stopped in front of a doorway just as it *whoosh*ed open and Data stepped out. The android was in the process of placing a madras porkpie hat on his head.

"Nice hat," said Beverly, looking past him and into the conference room, where she could see the captain, Will Riker, and other members of the command staff, plus half a dozen lower echelon officers. Deanna was right, only the two of them had been left out.

Data removed the hat and stuck it under his arm. "A souvenir for Spot."

The doctor looked pointedly at Captain Picard. "Well, we have souvenirs, too. Why weren't we invited?"

"That was my decision," said the captain, stepping forward. He opened his mouth and started to explain, then noticed the dozen crew members standing nearby.

"Sixteen hundred hours, docking bay twenty-seven," he told them. "Dismissed."

They left, although Will Riker took a long look at Deanna Troi and whispered, "Great dress."

"Come in," offered the captain, ushering the doctor and the counselor into the conference room. He pointed to the food slot. "Would you like anything?"

"We didn't mean to intrude," said Beverly, "if this was a private meeting."

The captain cleared his throat. "Let me explain.

There is to be a test mission in the hull section while the bridge is being repaired. We only needed fourteen volunteers, and it was left up to me who to ask. Of course, the first fourteen I asked volunteered. I'm sorry the two of you feel left out, but it was my determination that you need your shore leave, and neither one of you is crucial to this mission. We won't have a sickbay, but Martinez is a medic and will be properly equipped."

Briefly, he told them about the prototype saucer section and how it would crash-land on a planet and lift itself into the atmosphere to be grabbed by a tractor beam. It almost sounded convincing to Beverly, especially the part about needing only a skeleton crew, but she wasn't sure that Jean-Luc had entirely convinced himself.

"Are you sure you don't need a doctor on this mission?" she asked.

He tried to sound reassuring. "We're not going far, only to Kitjef II, and we'll be in contact with the starbase the whole time. I'm hoping only Data will be needed to fly the saucer section during planetary reentry. I was hesitant at first about this mission, but as long as Starfleet is determined to test their prototype, we might as well be the ones to test it. We do have a hull section that isn't being used."

"All right," said Beverly, rising to her feet. "But please be careful."

Counselor Troi shook her head adamantly. "Captain, why should you be deprived of your shore leave? These fourteen people are among the most overworked personnel on the ship, the ones who most need shore leave. I may lodge an official complaint with the admiral."

"Please do," said the captain with a smile. Picard picked up his duffel bag and started for the door, stopping long enough to say, "As a personal favor to me, try to enjoy your shore leave. Both of you need it and deserve it. You're not going to be missing out on much."

"Only your company," remarked Beverly.

"Yes, sorry about that." Looking as if he truly was sorry, the captain nodded curtly and strode off down the corridor.

"He has more reservations about this mission than he's telling us," said the Betazoid. "He didn't give us a chance to volunteer because he's *protecting* us."

The doctor nodded in agreement. "I know. At least he's taking Martinez. Well, there's nothing we can do but hope they pull it off, and hope that nothing goes wrong."

"Hope that nothing goes wrong," Deanna repeated, not sounding convinced. She checked the time. "Would you like to go hear a Bynar octet? The concert is just starting."

Beverly managed a polite smile. "Why not?"

Captain Slarn nodded patiently and pressed his fingers together, and Captain Picard detected just a trace of sympathy around his gray eyes, which was quite a compliment from the elder Vulcan. Slarn was one hundred and eighty years old and was known to run a tight starbase, although in practice, 211 seemed more freewheeling than most bases.

Captain Picard had begun his visit wanting to explain why he and so many of his staff would not be available to confer on the bridge repairs. Now he was deep into a recounting of the incident with the Pakled freighter.

The venerable Vulcan raised his hand to halt the story, and Picard was happy to oblige. "The rest is immaterial and reflects your needless angst over this affair. Suffice to say, Captain, you did nothing out of the ordinary. We are at a considerable disadvantage in our dealings with the Maquis. We do not wish to kill them or further alienate them, but we have allied ourselves against them. From their perspective, we betrayed them, and now they feel entitled to betray us."

The old Vulcan gazed at the stars through his circular window, which was too small to be much more than a peephole into infinity. "I have a kinsman serving on the Cardassian border, and he occasionally sends me reports. He is more optimistic about the situation than I am, but he is also considerably younger. Containing the Maquis sounds like dangerous work with little statistical chance of success. If our overriding goal is peace with Cardassia, then the logical course of action would be to help the Cardassians eliminate the Maquis. The needs of the many outweigh the needs of the few."

Picard scratched his chin. "We aren't ready to give up on the Maquis yet, but I admit, we can't give them what they really want—the territories we ceded to the Cardassians."

The Vulcan raised an eyebrow. "On the other

hand, much can be said for the theory that Cardassians are incapable of living in peace, and therefore our attempts to appease them are misguided. This is one instance where I do not envy those who are setting Starfleet policy."

"Neither do I," said Picard, thinking about his upcoming mission. He couldn't recall another time in his Starfleet career when he had been given two such undesirable assignments in a row, but border patrol and crash-landing a saucer section certainly qualified. It was always possible that both missions might surprise him and turn out to be rewarding, but he rather doubted it.

Captain Slarn glanced at his computer screen. "Everything is in readiness on dock twenty-seven. My operations officer assures me that you have enough room to separate the hull section while leaving the saucer section docked."

"That's reassuring," answered Picard, trying to keep the concern out of his voice. "And the prototype saucer?"

"They're in sensor range, proceeding at full impulse. ETA is thirty-nine minutes." The Vulcan rose from behind his desk, looking frail but hearty. "At least, Captain Picard, do not worry about your bridge. We'll have the baryon sweep and the repairs done and the new modules in place in forty-eight hours maximum. I'm afraid this won't be a newer version of the bridge equipment; in operation, it will be exactly the same as your old bridge."

Picard grinned with relief. "That will be splendid. Thank you."

Slarn tapped a panel, and his office door slid

open. "Shall we be going? I know that Admiral Nechayev does not like to be kept waiting."

"Uh, do you know her well?" asked Picard, leading the way into the corridor.

"The admiral?" The Vulcan paused in thought. "Answering that would require a definition of 'knowing someone well.' I know the admiral well enough to have formed opinions of her."

"Such as?"

"Admiral Nechayev is a very able officer," answered Slarn. "She is dedicated, intelligent, and driven. She was my commanding officer at the Ganymede colony twenty-eight years ago. Nechayev is one of the most direct humans I have ever met—one would almost think she was raised a Vulcan. Like most of my race, I hold her in the highest regard."

Only half in jest, Picard asked, "What's the secret to getting along with her?"

"Never make a mistake."

Picard sighed. "I thought as much."

The Vulcan brushed past him into the turbolift, and Picard dutifully followed. A few minutes later, they strode through the vast terminal, with its domed ceiling that sparkled with a simulation of meteors streaking across the heavens. The sight of so many excited travelers lifted Picard's spirits and made him realize that they would return to Starbase 211, if not this journey then sometime.

The captain smiled in greeting at Riker, Data, La Forge, Worf, Tate, and the other handpicked members of his volunteer crew, most of whom had beaten him to dock 27.

"May I introduce the commander of Starbase 211, Captain Slarn," he offered. There were polite greetings and a bit of small talk, but Picard found himself looking anxiously at his timepiece. He was still carrying his duffel bag, not having had time to unpack on the starbase, and he wondered if he would be able to find an exact duplicate of his quarters on the prototype saucer section.

"I would have expected Admiral Nechayev to see us off," he remarked.

Riker nodded in the opposite direction. "There she is now."

Everyone turned to see the sandy-haired admiral striding toward them, followed by a slim, dark-haired man who was limping slightly. *That must be her new aide,* thought Picard. He was wearing an electronic brace on his right knee, and the sleek, black apparatus pulsed with an occasional blip of light. The captain wondered whether the man had an artificial knee. At any rate, the man was wearing a cranberry-colored Starfleet uniform and the pips of a commander. With his limp and the bags he was carrying, he struggled to keep up with the energetic Nechayev.

Nechayev nodded curtly to the assembled crew. "At ease. I'm glad to see you're all on time. This is my aide, Commander Henry Fulton. This is Captain Picard, Commander Riker . . ." She went on to introduce all the crew members she knew, and Picard completed the introductions.

Captain Slarn gave the admiral a polite bow. "I hope nothing unfortunate has befallen your previous aide, Commander Rightwell."

For an instant, Nechayev looked wistful. "Rightwell was with me for eighteen years, but he needed a position with less stress and less travel. Besides, I have more and more long-term planning to do, and Commander Fulton is excellent with computer models and simulations. Wait until you see what he has cooked up for the simulated attack."

"I can hardly wait," said Picard with a brave smile. "Do you have equipment for us in those bags?"

"Hardly," answered Fulton. "We have clothes and toiletries, same as you."

"Clothes," repeated Picard. He stole a look at Admiral Nechayev, who was waiting expectantly for him to reach the inevitable conclusion. "You're coming with us?"

"Did I forget to mention that?" asked Nechayev with a smile. "I wouldn't miss this for the universe." She turned to the Vulcan. "I only wish you were coming with us, Slarn. I could always use another steady hand."

"There is considerable work to occupy me here." The commander took a step back and held up his hand in the traditional Vulcan greeting. "Live long and prosper."

"Thank you." Admiral Nechayev nodded and marched up the ramp toward the airlock, with Fulton struggling after her. Worf, Data, and the others followed suit, leaving Picard and Riker alone on the dock.

"Number One," said Picard grimly, "I have a special mission for you. It requires your unique talents."

The bearded officer nodded gamely. "You want me to charm Admiral Nechayev and keep her happy."

Picard grimaced slightly. "Let us say, you will be my special liaison to the admiral. You take charge of her, and I'll do my best to make sure we don't make any mistakes."

Timothy Wiley lay sleeping on a threadbare mattress in a storage room on the devastated planet of New Hope, only he dreamed he was in an officer's stateroom aboard a seagoing yacht, swaying in a hammock with the rolling of the ship. Unlike the burnt-rubber stench of New Hope, his dream locale had a bracing, salty aroma. Instead of subterranean darkness, there was sunlight streaming through white shutters.

He rustled in his hammock and didn't hear the maid creep into his stateroom until she was leaning over him, her scent mingling with that of the sea. She stroked his chest with her supple hands and tried to arouse him.

"Come on," she said softly. "Wake up."

Wiley thought he recognized her voice, but he knew he must be dreaming. He reached drowsily for the apparition only to encounter a hand of flesh and bone. With surprise, he ran his hand up her arm to her strong shoulder and her smooth neck and cheek.

She gently removed his hand. "You have to leave."

It was *the Architect,* thought Wiley. He reached

49

for her muscular shoulders. "One kiss, please. To remember why we're doing this."

The Architect pulled out of his grasp and stood up, her slim figure silhouetted in a crack of light from the doorway. "The freighter has returned ahead of schedule. Your success against the *Enterprise* has moved up the next phase of the plan. You've got to go immediately."

Wiley scrambled to his feet, buttoning his shirt. "I'd like to see you again! I'll try to come back."

"There's no guarantee I'll still be here," answered the Architect. "A messenger is waiting for you on the surface. Don't delay." With that last admonition, she was gone.

Timothy Wiley swallowed hard, worried that he might never see the lovely Bajoran again. If war was hell, it was also a strange sort of heaven, too, where scattered moments became magnified in intensity. He knew he wouldn't forget the Architect, and that he would try to get back someday to this hellhole.

Chapter Four

CAPTAIN PICARD GAZED AROUND the battle bridge, which was eight decks below the docking latches joining the saucer to the hull. There were the familiar stations—Ops, Conn, Weapons, Communications, plus programmable consoles—all within half the space of the main bridge. Unlike the main bridge, which was arranged in a horseshoe fashion with the crew's attention directed toward the main viewing screen, the battle bridge was circular and had smaller viewing screens. Because this was the battle bridge, there was an auxiliary weapons console and more instruments for tactical analysis. Worf was content, but the battle bridge reminded Picard of a stage in the round, something you built when you didn't have room for a real stage. Even more than the spaciousness of the main bridge, he missed having his ready room close at hand.

The captain stepped down from the command chair and straightened his tunic. He saw familiar faces: Data on Ops, Worf on Tactical, Tate on Conn, plus three backup crew members monitoring the separation systems. Riker had already spirited Admiral Nechayev and Commander Fulton down to Engineering, where La Forge and his team were at least operating in a normal environment. A third team from the skeleton crew was circulating among the life-support stations and transporter rooms, ready to pitch in where needed.

Knowing that he could fly the hull section just about anywhere and do battle with anything didn't assuage the captain's concerns. It only made him depressed to think that the saucer section—and the hundreds of civilians and nonessential crew it represented—was somehow expendable to the *Enterprise*. Had he endangered their lives needlessly over the years by not evacuating them more often? That was Nechayev's conclusion, and no one would ever be able to prove or disprove it. Perhaps a saucer separation drill would do him and his crew some good. In any case, the ship wouldn't be fragmented for long. It would rejoin with the prototype saucer only a few minutes after separating from its regular saucer. The captain tried to tell himself that he shouldn't complain about an opportunity to test-drive the latest model.

Resolutely, he tapped his comm badge. "Bridge to Engineering. Report, Mr. La Forge."

"Warp engines at one hundred percent, impulse engines at one hundred percent. Docking latches, thrusters, all separation systems check out. Everything looks fine from here."

The captain nodded. "Thank you, stand by. Picard to Martinez."

"Martinez here."

"What is your location?"

"I'm at the Oxygen Filtration station on deck twenty-two," came the reply. "Environmental controls appear to be functioning normally."

"Very well. All hands prepare for saucer separation." The captain nodded to Worf. "Open a channel to starbase operations."

"Yes, sir," answered the Klingon. "Channel open."

Picard looked at one of the viewers and saw the impassive face of Captain Slarn. The elder Vulcan was dwarfed by a glittering display behind him, which represented the extensive docking bays of Starbase 211. It reminded Picard of the *Enterprise*'s stellar cartography room.

"Captain," said the Vulcan, "you are free to disembark. We have routed traffic away from the station for the next seven-point-three minutes, and you may select whichever course is most convenient. Proceed when ready."

Captain Picard gave him a brief smile. "Thank you for your hospitality. I'm sorry a few of us didn't have more time to enjoy it."

"We will be here when you return," answered Slarn, "and your bridge will be operational again. Starbase 211 out."

Captain Picard leaned over Ensign Tate's shoulder and looked at her readouts. "Ensign, lay in course ninety mark one seventy. At my command, proceed at one-third impulse power."

"Aye, sir," answered the young officer as she entered the coordinates.

The captain glanced at Data. "Initiate separation sequence."

"Yes, sir." Nimbly the android entered commands at his console, and they felt a palpable shudder accompanied by a metallic thud. Data reported, "Latches retracting, thrusters on. Two thousand meters separation, six thousand meters, ten thousand meters."

The captain nodded at Tate. "Proceed."

As they changed course and pulled farther away, Picard leaned over a screen and personally changed the settings to show a view of his vessel speeding away from the starbase. No matter how many times he saw the hull section by itself, it looked odd, like the grip of some exotic weapon minus the barrel. The twin nacelles made the hull look rear-heavy without the saucer section to level the mass. Split in two, it just wasn't the *Enterprise,* decided the captain.

"Captain," said Data, "sensors are picking up the prototype saucer section. Its ETA at full impulse is nine point six minutes."

"Right on time," remarked Picard, nodding with approval. "They've come a long way without warp drive. Who's in command, I wonder. Hail them, Mr. Worf."

"Yes, sir."

A few seconds later, Picard found himself looking at a young Benzite lieutenant with blue skin and a breathing apparatus attached to his chest. With a soft hiss, the apparatus released gases into his nostrils, and his fishlike face beamed with delight. "Hello, Captain Picard, do you remember me? Perhaps you will mistake me for someone else of my geostructure."

The captain wagged his finger thoughtfully like an old schoolteacher. "Mendon, isn't it? Or should I say *Lieutenant* Mendon. Life in Starfleet must be agreeing with you."

"It is, Captain. I have gotten some of the most interesting assignments."

"Are you and your crew coming with us on this test flight?" asked Picard.

The Benzite moved his head awkwardly from side to side in a poor imitation of a shake. "No, sir. We've been promised shore leave."

"I see," answered Picard, his lips thinning. "Enjoy it, Lieutenant, you never know when you'll get the next one."

"Yes, sir. If you're ready to take command, we're ready to dock?"

The captain glanced at the Ops station. "Data has coordinates for you. In fact, I'd like Commander Data to beam over and handle it from your end."

The Benzite didn't hide his surprise at this slight. "Is that really necessary, sir? We are familiar with the reconnection procedure."

"I'm sure you are," said Picard with a diplomatic smile, "I just don't want anything to go wrong."

"Sending coordinates," said Data. After punching in the last command, the android rose to his feet, and another crew member took his place at Ops.

"Commander Data is on his way. *Enterprise* out." Picard frowned slightly at his final words, realizing that he really represented only *half* the *Enterprise*.

Picard tapped his comm badge. "Bridge to Martinez. Meet Commander Data in transporter room seven."

"Yes, sir."

The door to the turbolift *whoosh*ed open, and the android was about to exit when the captain called after him, "Mr. Data!"

"Yes, Captain."

"For all practical purposes, the saucer section is under your command. I don't need to tell you how important it is that every step of this operation goes without a hitch."

The android nodded. "Understood, Captain. Do you have reason to believe the operation might not go as planned?"

"No, I think we'll be fine." The captain smiled gamely and glanced at Worf and the young crew members manning the battle bridge. All command officers drilled regularly on the battle bridge, but had they drilled enough? Was there anything they were failing to take into account?

He finally shook his head. "Proceed, Mr. Data. Helm, take us to the rendezvous coordinates, half impulse."

* * *

In the Engineering control center deep in the bowels of the hull section, Will Riker glanced cautiously at Admiral Nechayev and her aide, Commander Fulton. He kept wondering if there was anything he should be doing to entertain them or otherwise enrich their experience. In the early going, they seemed content to watch the voyage unfold on the master situation monitor, a huge wall display. They conferred quietly between themselves, and he wasn't about to interrupt them. The first officer felt a bit guilty about being in Engineering with the captain alone on the bridge commanding a skeleton crew, but he kept reminding himself that he was here under captain's orders.

So Riker seated himself at a spare console and tried to look busy while he watched his charges. Admiral Nechayev was imprinted indelibly upon his mind, but her assistant was an unknown quantity. His predecessor, Rightwell, had been one of the most outgoing, helpful officers in the fleet, and he had meshed well with Nechayev's blunt style. After so many years with the admiral, Rightwell had had the confidence and ease to be his own man. Henry Fulton was too bookish for Riker's taste, and he spent too much time toadying up to the admiral, nodding exuberantly at her every word. To be fair, he was probably new at the job and thought that fawning was a prerequisite.

Admiral Nechayev pointed at the situation display. "Somebody just beamed off the ship? What is that about?"

Geordi walked past Riker giving him a sly smile, as if to say that answering an admiral's questions was a job for the first officer. Riker shifted in his chair and said, "The captain planned to beam Data over to the saucer to supervise the docking."

Nechayev narrowed her eyes at him. "He doesn't have confidence in the crew I assigned to pilot the prototype?"

"I'm sure that's not the case," said Riker with a mollifying smile. "He wants to make absolutely certain that nothing goes wrong. So he's putting Data in command of the saucer section."

"The idea of this mission is to test saucer separation under *normal* circumstances," snapped the admiral. "Or at least normal *emergency* circumstances. No other starship in the fleet can count on having a remarkable android like Data on hand. For a fair test, humans—or the equivalent—will have to command the saucer section."

"Yes, sir," agreed Riker, straightening in his chair.

"Tell me something else," said Nechayev, "is it standard procedure on the *Enterprise* for the first officer to be in Engineering during a mission?"

"Uh, no." The commander searched deep in his personality for some shred of charm that would work on the dour admiral. He finally decided upon honesty. "The captain wanted your concerns and questions to be addressed immediately, so he assigned me to you as liaison."

Her jaw tightened. "I don't need a liaison. I am perfectly capable of speaking directly to Captain Picard."

"Of course," said Riker.

"You know, Commander, Captain Jellico had

some very interesting things to say about you in his report, concerning the period when he commanded the *Enterprise*. I would like to discuss them with you when we have a moment."

Riker began to say something, but decided against it.

"Admiral," said Henry Fulton suddenly, "our models show that only four people are required to pilot the saucer section through reentry and landing. Most of it is automated. In an emergency situation, people will be thrust into unfamiliar stations, and the most experienced officers will probably carry the load. Therefore, may I suggest that the saucer have an experienced crew, such as the two of us, Commander Riker, and Commander La Forge."

The first officer tried not to let his jaw hang open. Luckily, Nechayev turned away from him, and he was able to relax for a moment. He gave Commander Fulton a grateful nod for changing the subject, even though Fulton's idea of a crew seemed less than ideal. Nevertheless, he owed the bookish officer one. Riker finally decided to let somebody else take control of Admiral Nechayev, as he wasn't up to the task.

He didn't dare object when the admiral said, "Very well, it will be the four of us in the saucer. I want to see for myself how well the new systems operate." She looked back at Riker. "I will speak to Captain Picard personally, and *you* will be in command of the saucer."

The commander nodded enthusiastically, not unlike Henry Fulton had behaved a few minutes earlier. "With pleasure, Admiral. May I say, I'm looking forward to the challenge."

"All hands prepare to dock," called Captain Picard over the shipwide intercom. Riker felt a twinge of guilt at having given in so easily to the admiral, but he doubted he was the first or would be the last to do so.

Commander Fulton clasped his hands together with approval. "I'm sure we're going to make an outstanding team. With this mission, I feel as if we're going to make history!"

"Docking complete," reported the Ops officer.

Captain Picard looked around at his young crew and nodded. "Well done. Remain here until I've transferred command to the main bridge."

The captain strode from the cramped battle bridge into the turbolift. "Bridge!" he barked at the computer.

He braced himself to stop abruptly if the turbolift tubes were not fully connected, but he felt the sensation of picking up speed as the lift raced through the saucer section. The doors slid open, and he stepped onto a bridge that was identical to his own, except that the lighting was a bit more subdued than he preferred. Lieutenant Mendon snapped to attention, as did six subordinates, all dressed in red command uniforms. Commander Data merely moved from the Conn station to his usual place at Ops.

"Welcome aboard, Captain," the Benzite said, beaming. "It was a pleasure to have Commander Data on the bridge, assisting us."

"I've always found that to be true," agreed the captain. He looked around at the spanking new bridge. "So how does she handle?"

The Benzite lowered his voice. "To be honest, sir, without the hull section she's a bit sluggish. After all, she is only half a ship."

"I agree with you," remarked Picard, "but let's not discuss that around Admiral Nechayev."

"Understood, sir. If there's nothing else, I'm prepared to turn command over to you."

"Make it so."

"Computer, transfer all command codes to Captain Jean-Luc Picard. Voice authorization—Mendon Epsilon six."

"Transfer complete," said the calm voice of the computer. "Hybrid prototype NCC-4011 is now under the command of Captain Jean-Luc Picard."

"I relieve you, Lieutenant," said the captain.

"I stand relieved."

Picard jutted his jaw. "Computer, transfer all command functions to the main bridge."

"All command functions transferred," answered the feminine voice. "Battle bridge is in standby mode."

The captain permitted himself a smile. "Catchy name for a ship—'hybrid prototype NCC-4011.' I hope we don't have to identify ourselves very often."

The Benzite snorted with laughter into his gas apparatus, and Picard chuckled as the turbolift doors *whoosh*ed open and Nechayev strode out, followed by Commanders Riker and Fulton. She

61

gave their laughter a fishy stare. They sobered immediately.

"Good job, Lieutenant," she said, turning to Mendon and his crew. I intend to commend each of your crew in my report."

"Why, thank you, sir."

"Lieutenant, how long has it been since you slept?"

The Benzite shrugged. "About fifty hours, I would say. I don't need much more than that."

"That is why I chose you for this assignment." Nechayev gave Picard a superior smile. "I always choose people very carefully for assignments."

The turbolift door opened, and Worf led the crew from the battle bridge onto the main bridge, where they took up their usual stations, with the Klingon at Tactical and Tate at the Conn.

"Have you turned over command to Captain Picard?"

"Yes, sir."

"Then enjoy your shore leave." Admiral Nechayev graced them with a fleeting smile.

"Lieutenant, we have an operator standing by in transporter room seven."

"Thank you, sir." The Benzite and his crew filed happily toward the turbolift, and Picard wondered what good deeds they had done to deserve such a quick escape.

"Captain," said Admiral Nechayev, "may we speak with you for a moment?"

"Certainly, my ready room." Without thinking, he strode confidently toward his office, and the door slid open as always. He stepped into a room that was devoid of desk, chairs, instruments, wall hangings, even a food slot. There was no fish tank, no familiar books or personal belongings.

"Perhaps Ten-Forward would provide a more congenial atmosphere." There was no reason not to be in a good mood, he decided, as everything seemed to be going well. "Helm, set a course for Kitjef II. As soon as Lt. Mendon and his crew have beamed off, we can depart. Number One, you have the bridge."

"Yes, sir," said Riker, also sounding very chipper.

Picard escorted the admiral and her aide to the lounge on deck ten. He was prepared to find Ten-Forward empty, without the tables, counters, customers, and bustling servers, but he wasn't prepared to find that they hadn't even installed viewing windows. Ten-Forward was nothing but a big empty space with walls coated a sterile white, not the vibrant starscape that he had expected.

"We haven't finished the nonessential interiors," said Henry Fulton. "I believe deck five has one wing of crew quarters. We plan to finish the rest after the test."

"If the saucer survives," added Picard.

Admiral Nechayev bounced on the balls of her feet. "It will. Captain Picard, I had a little discussion with Commander Riker, and there is no need for him to waste his time chaperoning us when we have only sixteen people on board."

"I see," said Picard. With a sinking feeling, he moved toward the door. "Would you like to see something else of the ship?"

"No. Commander Riker also told me about your plan to put the saucer section under Commander Data's control. I cannot approve that as it skews the test—only the *Enterprise* has a crewperson with Data's capabilities. Ideally, the saucer section should be commanded by regular line officers. To that end, the crew on the saucer will consist of myself, Fulton, Riker, and La Forge, with Riker commanding."

"Sir," said Picard tightly, "permission to speak freely?"

Her gray eyes glinted at him. "No, Captain, in this instance, you are *not* allowed to speak freely. I'm sure you will tell me that having Data alone on the saucer is the least risk of life, and I can't deny that. But we're only going to do this test once, and if humans are going to screw it up, then we need to know it now. Perhaps you want to tell me not to risk *my* life, but you insisted upon this being a volunteer mission—and *I'm* volunteering."

"Yes, sir," said Picard, pinning his shoulders back.

Nechayev's expression softened into what was almost a smile. "Besides, if you were really going to pilot the hull section into a dangerous situation, you would want Data with you. Isn't that true?"

"I suppose," Picard conceded, "and Riker would probably command the saucer section."

"You see, we are actually in agreement." The admiral turned to her aide and gazed at him like a doting aunt. "Commander Fulton has done an excellent job programming the computer simulation. I believe the attack that precipitates the saucer separation will be very realistic. The program is already in the ship's computer, is it not?"

"Yes, sir," answered Fulton with boyish pride. "I think the captain will have some difficulty defeating it."

Picard tried to sound cheerful as he asked, "Do I get to know who the foe is?"

Fulton glanced at his superior, but she folded her arms in front of her as if to let him carry the ball. "Here is the scenario," he began. "You receive a distress call from a colony on Kitjef II saying they are under attack, and you are the closest ship to them. Naturally, you respond. How soon would you be able to ascertain the problem, find out who the attacker is?"

Crisply the captain responded, "Long-range sensors would give us some idea immediately, and we would keep trying to contact the colony for more information. It's a short hop at maximum warp."

"Understood," said Nechayev, studying him intently. "If you saw that it was an all-out, merciless attack—with no previous hostilities reported in that sector—who would you think was responsible?"

Picard met her gaze, thinking she was quite a remarkable woman even if she was infuriating. She was Starfleet's idea of an avenging angel, there was no doubt about that.

"The Borg," he answered softly.

She smiled. "That is correct. Before you suggest that this is some sort of punishment, let me tell you that the simulation was programmed long before you cracked up your bridge. We expected to use the

65

hull of the *Bolivar,* but she won't be finished for another couple months yet."

The admiral folded her hands in front of her, looking pleased. "With your special knowledge of the Borg, you will probably stand a better chance of defeating this scenario than anyone else."

"Why would I crash-land the saucer on the very planet they're attacking?"

"You'll see," said Nechayev with a smile. "Fulton and I will be returning to Engineering. Please notify me as soon as we reach Kitjef II."

"Yes, sir."

With that, the admiral and her aide walked out and headed for the turbolift. The captain rubbed his eyes and gazed around the empty cavern that was simply a room, not a lounge, on this prototype vessel. He wished Guinan were here.

Picard let his superior get a considerable head start before leaving Ten-Forward, then he turned the opposite way in the corridor. He went down to the nearly deserted hull section and retrieved his duffel bag from a locker. At a computer terminal, he asked the computer to tell him where his quarters were, and he wasn't surprised to hear they were on deck five.

The simple, unadorned crew quarters were adequate, especially since he didn't have time to actually rest. The captain merely wanted to dump his duffel bag and see a working food slot.

The captain sat on the bunk near the replicator and massaged his stomach for a moment before ordering, "Tea, chamomile, lukewarm."

Chapter Five

THE TURBOLIFT DOORS OPENED, and Will Riker's head turned along with everyone else's to see who would step off. When Captain Picard emerged alone and the doors slid shut behind him, the crew seemed to relax. Worf nodded curtly in welcome, and the first officer vacated the command chair to allow the captain to sit.

He bent low and whispered, "Captain, that special assignment you gave me . . ."

Picard held up his hand. "Some forces in the universe are beyond our control."

"Exactly." The first officer straightened his back. "Data, how soon until we get there?"

"Approximately seventeen point two minutes," answered the android.

The captain frowned as if he had eaten something distasteful. "I've been given the scenario for our simulated battle. We are answering a distress call from a mythical colony on Kitjef II. Data, give us a brief abstract on Kitjef II."

The android swiveled deftly in his seat and replied, "The Kitjef system was discovered in 2151 by the *Alamo,* an early, multigenerational exploration vessel. It was the third generation who discovered the system and named it after their most recently born children, Kit Carson and Jefferson Davis. Hence, Kitjef. None of the seven planets are inhabited, but the second planet is class M. Kitjef II was briefly mined for uranium, but the mines were deserted when superior energy sources became available. Today Kitjef II is again uninhabited with only lichens and grubs in abundance. It has been used many times for Federation training and test missions."

The captain scratched his jaw. "What do they want?"

"What do *who* want?" asked Riker.

"The Borg," answered Picard. "That's our adversary in this simulation."

The first officer shook his head at the irony of it. "Life has a way of testing us, doesn't it, sir?"

"Number One," said the captain gravely, "I'm depending upon you to get the saucer down in one piece."

"Understood, sir. I intend this to be one we'll walk away from."

The turbolift doors opened again, and Admiral Nechayev and Commander Fulton strode onto the bridge. The admiral took a stance near the command chair with her hands behind her back, as if she were bracing for battle. Commander Fulton took a rear position near Worf, where he had plenty of spare consoles to peruse. Riker tensed, waiting for the inevitable.

"Fifteen minutes and counting to arrival," said the admiral. "Have you informed your crew of the situation?"

Picard cleared his throat and touched a panel on his armrest. "Attention, all hands, this is Captain Picard. We are approximately fifteen minutes away from our destination. As soon as we come out of warp drive, we will begin the simulated attack. Our foe is a Borg ship. Be prepared to report to battle stations. Commander La Forge, we need you on the bridge. Picard out."

The captain looked at his first officer. "Actually this is the point at which Commander Riker often informs me that saucer separation is one of our options."

"Commendable," answered Nechayev. "And what do you usually say?"

"I usually say I will take it under advisement. This being the Borg, I would give the suggestion more thought. In fact, I suggest we come out of warp at the outer edge of the solar system and use long-range sensors to see what's happening."

Nechayev nodded with approval and looked at her aide. "As you predicted."

The turbolift doors opened, and Geordi walked onto the bridge. "Reporting for duty, Captain."

"Take your regular station, Mr. La Forge. When we separate, you'll be part of the saucer crew."

Geordi nodded as if he half expected that to happen. He crossed behind Worf's tactical station and went to his Engineering console. The crew person there moved over to the Science station.

For the next fifteen minutes, they went through level three diagnostics on the separation systems, making sure everything was in readiness. Riker spent the time reviewing in his mind the procedures for piloting a saucer section into planetary atmosphere and landing it.

Piloting was not the correct word as the computer would do most of that, making minute course corrections based upon the planet's atmosphere, soil composition, and terrain. The new dampeners and forcefields were completely automated, or so he had been assured.

Kitjef II was your basic rock, he reminded himself, with nary a tree and only a handful of mountains, which they ought to be able to avoid. As long as he stayed alert at the Conn, double-checking the course corrections, the saucer should be fine.

"We are coming out of warp," reported Data.

"Shields up," ordered Riker, thinking he might as well get into the spirit of things.

"Shields up," answered Worf.

"On screen," said Picard. "Full stop."

Space seemed to slow down as the stars on the viewscreen stopped streaking by and became glimmering beads in the starscape. A whitish planet that looked bleached of life filled the screen as Data narrowed the image on Kitjef II. It was hard to imagine that such a lifeless rock harbored a class-M atmosphere, but it had a low dew point and underground streams that kept moisture flowing despite the lack of real oceans.

"Long-range sensors reveal nothing abnormal on Kitjef II," reported Data.

"I believe it's time to start the simulation," said Admiral Nechayev. "You are aware how quickly a Borg vessel can move."

"I am aware," answered Picard. "We do have the standard safeguards on the program, don't we?"

"Of course," answered Henry Fulton, looking hurt at the suggestion that he could be negligent. "I'm sorry there wasn't time to explain the simulation to you in detail, Captain, but you'll soon be an expert. Shall we begin?"

"One moment," said Picard. "Attention, all hands, we are beginning the simulation that will result in the saucer separation. Even though this is a drill, the dangers are very real. So step lively, and be prepared for an actual emergency. Picard out."

"Was that really necessary?" asked Admiral Nechayev with mild annoyance.

The captain nodded. "Yes, it is. To all of us this looks like our regular ship, but I wanted to remind everyone that it really isn't. And I don't want anybody getting lackadaisical, thinking this is only a drill and they can walk through it. Commander Fulton, you may begin your simulation."

Riker glanced at the admiral, wondering how she would react to the captain's explanation. But Nechayev simply turned to a vacant station and began monitoring the separation systems.

Henry Fulton stood up, favoring the leg that did not have a brace. "Computer, begin simulation Proto-Borg eleven. Voice authorization—Fulton omega seven."

"Bridge controls transferred to computer," the voice responded. Riker frowned. He didn't really like having the computer in total control, even if it was only temporary.

At once, the viewscreen filled with an enormous gray mass—a perfect cube dimpled with airlocks, vents, and alien machinery. It was the kind of apparition no sane person would expect to see in space. Riker gaped at the monstrous slab of machinery and reminded himself that it wasn't real.

"Reverse, full impulse!" shouted the captain, but it was too late as a searing beam issued from the cube and raked across the viewscreen. Automatically the piercing sound and blinking lights of a red alert came on.

"Shields down fifty percent!" shouted Worf.

Tate got the *Enterprise* moving from a dead stop in surprisingly quick time. They were streaking away in reverse as another blast from the Borg ship glanced off their shields and staggered everyone on the bridge. Riker knew from past experience that the early going was when you had the best chance of hurting a Borg vessel, before they modulated their shields to match your phaser frequencies. You got one free shot, maybe two if you varied your frequencies, and that was it. Was the captain going to take his shots now? He sure as hell couldn't outrun a Borg cube.

Picard strode closer to the Conn. "Evasive sequence beta one three."

"Yes, sir," answered Tate, never taking her eyes off her instruments.

The deck jerked abruptly, and Riker staggered to keep his balance. The Borg ship was fading in size as the *Enterprise* drew away, but he knew it could close the gap within seconds.

"Shields down to thirty-six percent," reported Data. "Some power fluctuations, but minimal damage to crucial systems. However, we cannot sustain another hit like the first one."

"Route auxiliary power to shields," ordered the first officer, wishing there was something else he could do. "They don't seem to be coming after us."

"Worf," said the captain, "hail the colonists on Kitjef II."

The Klingon raised an eyebrow at the prospect of hailing nonexistent colonists, but he performed his duty. He looked somewhat surprised when he reported, "The colonists have responded. I have their mayor."

"On screen."

A thin but vibrant-looking man with tufts of hair sprouting over his ears regarded them from some dark chamber that looked hewn from sheer rock. "This is Bill Cody," he panted. "Thank God you've come! Two cities have already been destroyed, and we're under attack!"

"Not at the moment," said Picard, "Because the Borg ship is battling us. This is Captain Jean-Luc Picard of the starship *Enterprise*. How were you spared?"

"I think it's because we're underground, in the old mines. Maybe they can't detect us down here. Thousands are dead, all over the planet, but they didn't come after us. Can you beam us out?"

Riker glanced at Nechayev but her expression gave no clue as to what she was thinking. "Our situation is more tenuous than yours. How did they attack? What did they seem to want?"

"People," said Bill Cody with a shudder. "They struck with incendiary missiles that drove everyone into the streets, then they beamed down with stun rifles. Horrible . . . horrible . . . they took them alive or dead, it didn't matter. My whole family was in one of those cities."

"We'll get help," promised Picard.

The captain evidently saw no reason to continue conversing with simulated colonists. "Starship out," he said. Then he paced the length of the bridge, addressing different crew members. "Helm, full impulse to Kitjef II. Continue evasive maneuvers. Worf, open a channel to Starfleet. Report the situation. Riker, begin evacuation into the saucer section." He glanced at Admiral Nechayev. "I believe our best time is about five minutes."

"Five minutes and twenty-four seconds," said Henry Fulton. "That's the time the program is allotting you."

On a spare console Riker entered the command to evacuate the ship. If this had been the real thing, he would have made a shipwide announcement himself, then rushed down to the hull to shepherd people into the turbolifts. Hell, they would all be doing that. Panic, uncertainty, frightened children, priceless belongings left behind—it was not something he wanted to see ever again. It helped him breathe easier to remember that this was only a drill.

Over the bridge's comm system, the computer's calm voice intoned, "Begin emergency evacuation. This is not a drill. Proceed to your emergency station in the saucer section. Begin emergency evacuation. This is not a drill."

Riker glanced at the captain. He wasn't sure what Captain Picard would really do in this hypothetical situation, but he could see the advisability of stopping the Borg ship now, before it could wreak havoc all over the sector.

"Starfleet has replied," said Worf. "The *Sparta* and the *Frederick* have been dispatched and will reach here in thirty minutes. Our primary orders are to save lives, and our secondary orders are to engage the Borg vessel and not let it escape from this solar system."

"Perhaps there's a way to do both," said Picard. "If the saucer section can land on the planet, they can take refuge with the survivors while we do battle. I think we can hold the Borg here until we get reinforcements."

"Bravo, Captain," said Henry Fulton, not hiding his amusement. "The simulation will get interesting for you after we leave, I promise."

Picard scowled slightly and looked at Data. "How are we doing on the evacuation?"

"Two minutes more," answered the android. "The Borg ship is scanning us."

Picard's jaw tensed. "Mr. Worf, report on shields and weaponry."

"Shields at forty-four percent," answered the Klingon. "Weapon systems at one hundred percent, with phasers set for automatic frequency shift. Captain, I anticipate having three shots— one with a photon torpedo and two with phasers— before the Borg ship adjusts its defenses. I could tell you more accurately from the battle bridge."

"Understood," said Picard. "It's time we all go down there. Computer, activate battle bridge."

"Battle bridge activated."

The captain held out his hand, and Will Riker took it. "Good luck to you, Number One. We have Borg to face, but they aren't real. The ground on Kitjef II is hard and real."

"I used to fly antique ultralights," answered Riker. "If I can land one of those, I can land this saucer."

Picard nodded, satisfied. He tapped his comm badge. "Attention, all hands, this is Captain Picard. Those assigned to the saucer section are Nechayev, Riker, La Forge, and Fulton. All personnel who are not assigned to the saucer section should report to their stations in the hull section. Prepare for saucer separation."

"Evacuation complete," said Data as he stood from his station. If he was surprised about being reassigned, he didn't show it.

Worf led the crew members into the turbolift, while Captain Picard paused for a moment in front of Admiral Nechayev. "I sincerely hope that your improved saucer works. I wouldn't mind seeing this bridge again."

"Thank you, Captain," she answered with a polite smile. "We will be toasting our success in a few hours."

The captain nodded and strode into the turbolift. "Battle bridge," he said grimly.

Riker turned around and surveyed his small crew, which consisted of a fellow commander, a lieutenant commander, and an admiral. He didn't know whether to break out laughing or crying. In reality, he supposed, it wasn't surprising that this was a privileged group; very few people would ever get to experience a roller coaster ride like this one.

He finally decided to make some assignments. "La Forge on Ops, Fulton on Science, Nechayev on Tactical, and I will take the Conn. As acting captain of this vessel, I expect you to follow orders as if you were back in the Academy."

"Of course," said Nechayev, bounding up to Worf's usual station. She looked good back there, legs at a wide stance, slim torso erect, hands hovering over the instruments. Fulton merely converted the station where he was already sitting to a detailed display of Kitjef II, including weather and atmospheric conditions. With a game smile, Geordi crossed in front of him and sat at Data's usual station. Riker knew that Geordi was an excellent pilot, especially when it came to navigation, which meant they could switch stations if that proved necessary.

The acting captain nodded with satisfaction and took his own seat at the Conn. He touched his badge. "Bridge to battle bridge. We're ready when you are."

There was a pause. "We are ready to proceed," answered Picard.

Riker leaned back in his chair and took a deep breath. "All hands ready?" His makeshift crew nodded back at him. "Begin saucer separation, Mr. La Forge."

Geordi entered the command, and for the second time that day, they heard the immense latches, servos, and umbilicals pull apart. The saucer lurched slightly as the thrusters kicked in. If all went well, thought Riker, they would go through reconnection in a few hours.

"We're free," said Geordi. "Four thousand meters separation."

"Going into standard orbital approach," announced Riker, as the pale planet loomed ever closer, taking up most of the viewscreen. "Fulton, is the computer reading data from the planet?"

"As fast as it can," answered the commander.

"Then I'll begin the search for an optimal orbit and reentry." Riker entered commands and nodded with satisfaction as the computer searched swiftly through all the possibilities. It computed an orbit that would decay into the proper deorbital trajectory. Suddenly, the viewscreen went blank and the lights blinked off for a moment.

"What the hell was that?" growled Riker.

"We were hit by a beam weapon from the Borg

78

ship," answered Geordi with amazement. "We're down to half impulse. Our computer is still tied in with the mock battle!"

"Turn that bloody thing off, Fulton!" shouted Riker. When he turned around, all he saw were the turbolift doors slamming shut.

"Fulton!" shouted Nechayev. "Come back here!" She looked apologetically at Riker. "I don't know what's gotten into him." She tapped her comm badge. "Nechayev to Fulton. Report back to the bridge immediately."

Riker made a quick decision. "As acting captain, I'm aborting this mission. Computer, end simulation."

The lights went out again as they were rocked by another imaginary shot. Red emergency low-power lights came back on, but the viewscreen went blank.

"Sir," said Geordi, "inertial dampers and gravitational grids are failing, at least in the simulation. I can't get control of the ship at all. None of the overrides are working!"

"Weapons systems down!" shouted Nechayev. "Shields buckling."

As if their minds reached the same conclusion at the same instant, Riker and Nechayev looked at one another then at the station Fulton had vacated only seconds earlier. On the floor near Fulton's chair was a metal ball about the size of an orange.

"Take cover!" shouted Riker as the concussion grenade exploded and ripped the air, throwing him off his feet.

His mind went as blank as the viewscreen overhead.

"The saucer section has been hit and is disabled," reported Data from the Ops console of the battle bridge.

Picard gave him a taut smile. "In the simulation, I trust."

Data frowned. "That is not readily apparent, Captain. As the saucer is part of the simulation, this information may be unreliable. According to my sensors, the saucer section has slowed to one-third impulse and is continuing erratically in its approach to the planet."

"Captain," said Worf with concern, "the Borg vessel is chasing after the saucer section. If we do not retaliate, they will be destroyed."

Picard wanted to forget about this; but he had agreed to play, and he had a duty to perform as well as he could under the circumstances. Still, it was high time they wrapped up this charade and got down to the real purpose of their mission.

"Target photon torpedo," he ordered, "and fire when ready."

"Targeting torpedo," said Worf. "Torpedo away."

The captain glanced at his screen in time to see the Borg ship take a direct hit. Green sparks rippled along the cube's surface. It stopped dead in space, which was the main idea.

A blinding blue beam streaked from the cube, struck the ship, and blanked Picard's viewer.

"Direct hit," said Data. "Shields down to three percent."

"Status of the saucer?"

The android shook his head. "Unable to report. Sensors damaged."

"That's quite enough of this," the captain declared angrily. "We need to know what's really happening with the saucer section. Computer, end simulation."

"The Borg ship is powering up," said Data.

"End program!" shouted Picard. "Voice authorization—Picard alpha six. Data, override the program and get control of the ship back."

The android's fingers flew over the console, but he shook his head. "Captain, I am unable to comply. The computer core in the battle bridge has been altered at the alpha level, as if by a virus. The safeguards have been erased, and the simulation has complete control of the hull's computer."

"Captain," said Worf urgently, "the Borg vessel is pursuing the saucer section again."

"Ready phasers. Fire at will," snapped the captain. "Data, there's got to be some way to stop this program."

"Direct hit!" announced Worf. "They are turning on us. Captain, may I suggest evasive action."

"Helm, evasive action, your sequence."

"Yes, sir," answered Ensign Tate.

Picard staggered to keep his balance as the ship made an abrupt maneuver. "Data, any suggestions?"

"Sir, we could do a core dump, but that would

take hours and require the main computer on the *Enterprise* saucer section, which we do not have."

Tight-lipped, the captain turned to Worf. "Hail the saucer section, emergency frequency."

The Klingon glowered at his instruments. "I am sorry, sir. After that last hit, our signal strength is erratic. I do not know if they are receiving our hail, but they do not respond."

"Data, what will happen if we simply let the Borg destroy us?"

Data looked at him, taking the question very seriously. "Judging from our experience so far, we cannot assume that defeat will return control to us. The surest and safest way to end the simulation would be to defeat the Borg vessel."

Picard stared past the android at the ominous cube on the viewer. It swiveled slowly in space, as if lining up another shot.

"Helm," he barked, "get us out of here, warp two. *Engage!*"

Chapter Six

"RETREAT, CAPTAIN?" ASKED WORF with surprise, once they had put a few light-years between themselves and the simulated Borg vessel. The Klingon wouldn't have considered retreat this early in the battle.

"Yes, retreat," answered the captain testily, "all the way back to Starbase 211, if this ridiculous program will let us. In fact, send a message to Starbase 211 that we are malfunctioning and are returning to base."

"Yes, sir," answered the Klingon. After a moment, he growled and banged his fist on the console. "They insist that we engage the Borg and hold them until reinforcements arrive, no matter what the condition of our vessel. All I am getting is the simulation!"

"Captain," said Data, "the Borg ship has entered warp drive and will overtake us in twelve point three seconds."

"Helm, bring us out of warp. Reverse course and take us back to Kitjef II at warp four. Don't give them time to catch us."

"Yes, sir," answered Tate.

His jaw clenched, Captain Picard stalked back and forth across the compact battle bridge. "You were right, Mr. Worf, retreat isn't really an option. We can't outrun them, and we have to find out what's happening with the saucer section. Data, is there any part of the ship that hasn't been taken over by this program?"

"The computer subsystems in the shuttlecraft should be unaffected," answered the android.

The captain leaned over Data's console and stared at the calm android. "Can we launch a shuttlecraft without getting it dragged into the simulation?"

"Yes," answered the android, "if we take the proper precautions. Any contact between the ship and the shuttlecraft might compromise the shuttle-craft's computer. A successful launch would involve one person manually opening the space doors while another person manually piloted the craft out. The computer would still take note of the shuttlecraft's launch and include it in the simulation. However, a shuttlecraft that was operating independently would not be affected by fire from the Borg ship."

"Precisely," said Picard. "Worf, you pilot the shuttlecraft. Find the saucer, get their status and location, and report back to us."

"Captain," said Data, "I would advise against any ship-to-ship contact in case the virus can travel on subspace frequencies. Until we stop this simulation, any action we take might have unforeseen consequences."

"All right," said Picard, "just find out what's going on. Data, go with him to open the space doors. You won't have tractor beams to guide you, Worf."

"I understand, sir."

Worf bulled his way into the turbolift and waited for Data to join him. "Shuttlebay three!" snarled the Klingon. He looked at Data and shook his head with frustration. "How could a training program take over our entire ship?"

"Actually, it is quite simple if you alter the safeguards built into the computer. I suspect very few memory locations are actually damaged. Unfortunately, the computer cannot discern the difference between what is real and what is imaginary, and it refuses to listen to us when we tell it."

The turbolift door opened, and Worf stepped out and took a sharp turn to the right. He began to jog down the deserted corridor, and Data kept perfect pace beside him. They dashed into shuttlebay three, the largest bay on the ship after the main shuttlebay, which unfortunately, was on the saucer section.

Out of habit, Worf glanced up at the control booth that overlooked the vast bay, but nobody was in the sealed chamber. So he turned his attention to the five shuttlecrafts. At any given time, three of the crafts in bay three were supposed to be operational, but the biggest shuttle, a Type 7 personnel carrier, was down for repairs. Only one other craft had warp drive, and that was the Type 6 carrier by the door; all the others were short-range shuttlepods. Even though the *Amundsen* didn't have phasers, it would have to do, because things were too dangerous out there to be caught without warp drive.

"Commander," asked Worf, "do we have time to install phasers on the *Amundsen?*"

Before the android could answer, the lights went out and emergency red lights blinked on, along with a fresh red alert. "No, we do not," answered Data, briskly moving toward the stairway that led up to the control booth.

"That is unfortunate." Worf pulled out the safety blocks around the landing rails of the *Amundsen* and banged on the panel that opened the hatch.

Data stopped outside the control booth and looked down at him. "I must turn off the tractor beams in order to make sure the shuttlecraft is not affected by the simulation. Can you see in this light?"

"I will use my landing lights." Worf ducked under the hatch and climbed aboard the shuttlecraft. He scurried between the six passenger seats and threw himself into the pilot's seat in the cockpit. Immediately, both his and the copilot's instrument panels blinked on. He left them on, welcoming the light because the shuttlebay had turned into an eerie cavern. As he went through his prelaunch checklist, he had to remember not to ask the hull's computer for any information, and he carefully turned off every automatic system in the shuttlecraft. There would be no contact or electronic guidance—this was going to be a pure solo flight.

The space doors opened without warning. Worf could see lights flickering above him in the immense docking bay, and he assumed that the captain was diverting emergency power to the shuttle-bay.

The Klingon turned on the shuttle's landing lights, which glinted off the walls. At the yawning door, the light was absorbed by the blackness of space. He lifted off, wobbly at first, and gritted his teeth at the sound of his landing rails scraping the deck. He was taking careful aim at the opening when he saw the doors start to shut. The simulation must have realized what was happening! With no time to think, Worf jammed the throttle forward and careened into a narrowing doorway.

The sleek craft scraped the space doors, sending sparks shooting off its hull, but it slipped through as the doors clanged shut. Worf struggled to right the shuttle, and he narrowly missed plowing into one of the nacelles. Finally, he gained control of the craft and veered away from the beleaguered hull section. The Klingon smiled grimly, imagining that the Borg ship was emptying its weapons at him without the slightest effect.

The pale, dead-looking planet of Kitjef II loomed large in his cockpit window. He put on the shuttle's sensors and searched for life-forms, knowing there would be none on the deserted planet except for the saucer crew. After an hour of circling the planet at much higher speeds than a normal orbit, there was no sign of life, the saucer section, or anything but the ruins of the old mines and the prefabricated villages that once supported them. Using his communication system was a risk, according to Data, but Worf realized that he had to try hailing the saucer. Several hails on standard frequencies produced no response.

Worf reached the conclusion that if the saucer had attempted reentry, it had either burned up in the atmosphere or crashed into smithereens. Either way, Riker, La Forge, Nechayev, and Fulton were dead, a prospect he wasn't eager to accept or report to the captain. Only a ship like the *Enterprise* would be able to search for the minute wreckage that might be left.

There were two other explanations for the saucer's disappearance, neither one of which brought him any comfort. One was that his shuttle-craft was, in fact, under control of the simulation, despite their precautions. The only other explanation was that the saucer had never landed on Kitjef II at all. Then where was it? Since the saucer only had impulse power, it couldn't have gone far, relatively speaking. Still, it would take days to scour the Kitjef solar system in a shuttlecraft, so reluctantly Worf headed back to the hull section.

He wasn't prepared for what he found: The hull section lay dead in space, tilted at an obscene angle, portholes and running lights dark. He raged inwardly at the senselessness of a great ship brought down by a nonexistent foe and a runaway computer program! He hadn't feared for his crewmates' lives when he left, but if the program had shut down life-support, they could all be dead, except for Data.

"Qa'Plah!" he cursed. "I will avenge you!"

Without any weaponry on the shuttlecraft, his options were limited, so he brought his shuttlecraft to a stop and opened a hailing frequency. "Worf to the hull section. Do not reply! If you are able, detonate a low-impact photon torpedo at the coordinates where the Borg ship is according to the simulation. Unfortunately, it will not harm them, but it will show me where they are. Worf out."

He waited tensely for a few seconds. Perhaps everyone, including Data, was incapacitated. Finally, the hull section launched a torpedo, and it exploded harmlessly about a hundred kilometers in front of the reported position of the Borg ship. With a growl, Worf set his course and made for the spot at full impulse.

Once again, he imagined the enemy ship's blistering fire as he streaked toward it. He could only hope that the shuttlecraft was still being received by the *Enterprise* hull's computer as part of the simulation, even if it couldn't be affected by it. If he really was tied into the simulation, then his death was only seconds away. But what a glorious way to die!

At full impulse, he plowed into empty space where the Borg ship should have been. Then he circled back to the hull section and waited. With considerable relief, he saw lights twinkle on up and down the hull and the twin nacelles, as the ship righted itself.

Picard's voice came over his radio. "Congratulations, Mr. Worf! You have single-handedly destroyed a Borg ship, and not a moment too soon. This is the first suicide mission I've ever seen anyone survive."

"Thank you, sir."

"Where is the saucer section?"

The Klingon groaned in frustration. "I am sorry, sir, but there is no sign of it."

He could hear the amazement in the captain's voice. "No sign of it? Are you sure?"

"It is a large planet, and my sensors are limited," Worf muttered in frustration. "Perhaps you would have better luck searching for it."

"Return to the ship immediately," ordered the captain. "We'll get to the bottom of this."

Will Riker felt as if somebody had been playing the timpani part from the "1812 Overture" on his skull. Not only that, but every muscle ached. He blinked his eyes at the blurry scene around him and tried to roll over, which was when he discovered that his hands were bound behind him and his feet were tied together.

As his mouth wasn't gagged, he started to shout. "What the hell's going on!"

"Now, now, Commander," said a calm voice, "you'll wake up your friends."

Riker squirmed around on the deck of the bridge until he could find the source of the voice. It was Henry Fulton, who was sitting in the command chair. Fulton pressed a button on his knee brace, and a small compartment slid open. From the compartment he took a phaser and trained it on Riker.

"My brace is handy for carrying things you're not supposed to have," he remarked. The first officer wriggled futilely until he spotted Geordi, who was still unconscious and bound hand and foot right on the deck. He lay where he had fallen near the Ops station.

Henry Fulton chuckled. "I would tell you to be quiet, but I don't suppose it matters if you make noise. The admiral is bound to drown you out when she wakes up."

Riker squirmed some more and found Admiral Nechayev lying near the Tactical station, in the same predicament. He tried to remain calm, telling himself that he wasn't in a position to be abusive to a man holding a phaser on him. So he gritted his teeth and tried to sound reasonable.

"What do you think you're going to accomplish?" he asked.

"A hijacking of the *Enterprise*," answered Fulton. "Or a reasonable facsimile thereof."

"You've only got half the *Enterprise*," said Riker, hoping that was true.

"So far." Fulton smiled and glanced over his shoulder. "Oh, I see the admiral is coming to. Excuse me, Commander, I've got to pay close attention to her."

Nechayev twisted around, immediately alert and fuming with anger. "What is the meaning of this? Release us this instant!"

Henry Fulton stood, favoring his good leg and looking highly amused. "Admiral, I'm afraid you're in no position to be giving orders. For twenty years, you've made everybody in Starfleet squirm. Nobody was good enough for you, nobody could measure up. Well, it's your turn to obey—it's your turn to toe the line or suffer the consequences."

"You son of a bitch!" Nechayev began flopping back and forth like a hooked fish in the bottom of a boat. She struggled against her bindings with such ferocity that Riker was afraid she would dislocate a shoulder.

"Stop that!" ordered Fulton. He moved toward her, leveling the phaser. "Don't make me hurt you. We don't want to hurt any of you."

"Who is *we?*" asked another voice, and Riker turned to see that Geordi had come to his senses, probably wishing he hadn't.

"The Maquis," answered Fulton with pride.

"Maquis!" gasped Nechayev. "Impossible!"

"I told you to keep quiet!" snapped Fulton, waving his weapon menacingly. "I don't want to stun you—I need you alert."

"Why?" she demanded.

"Because we're going to do something that none of the Federation's enemies have ever accomplished—stealing a Galaxy-class starship without firing a shot and without getting a scratch on it! Admiral, do you think *you're* important to the Maquis? Hardly. This ship is, and when it's whole, we'll be able to chase the Cardassians out of the DMZ forever!"

The admiral stopped struggling and just stared at her former aide. "Why *you?*" she asked. "You're throwing away your career, your whole life!"

"I wish that were true," said Fulton with a sigh. "But I haven't got the personality to rise any higher than a position as your errand boy, and you know it. Oh, I have some skills you find useful, but I was never going to command a ship or become an admiral, at least not in Starfleet. In the Maquis, I can command the *Enterprise* if I want."

"You're doing this for personal gain?" asked Riker.

The commander pointed the phaser at him. "Hardly. I'm doing this because the Federation has lost its way. It's grown soft, appeasing our enemies, repaying loyalty with treachery. You took our colonies away, sold us out to the Cardassians—*you're* the traitors!"

"Listen," said Riker, "you haven't got any chance of pulling this off. How far can you get this saucer without warp drive?"

"Plenty far," answered Fulton victoriously, "when the saucer is in a tractor beam of a ship that *does* have warp drive. We're already light-years away from Kitjef II, and by this time I'm sure that Captain Picard is very confused. Did you think I was acting alone? No, Commander. As the admiral told you, I'm good at long-term planning, and so are my comrades in the Maquis."

A chime on the Tactical console sounded, and Fulton climbed stiffly up the ramp, making sure not to get too close to Nechayev. Even bound hand and foot, she was still a formidable presence as she glared at him with abject hatred in her cold gray eyes.

The commander tapped a panel, and they all heard, "Shufola to Fulton. Come in, Fulton."

"Fulton here."

"We're coming out of warp on the edge of the Thresher Dust Cloud. Is everything under control?"

"Couldn't be better. We're ready for the next phase."

"Stand by," said the voice. "We'll beam our party over. Shufola out."

"Want to see where we are?" Fulton touched the console, and the main viewscreen lit up with eerie, magenta-colored swirls of dust, stretching over thousands of kilometers as far as the eye could see. Riker tried to remember what he knew about the Thresher Dust Cloud, a beautiful but desolate stretch of space that ships avoided because sensors and transporters malfunctioned within the ionized cloud. It was the perfect place for an ambush.

"If you think Captain Picard is going to walk into a trap," said Geordi, "you don't know him very well."

"He won't have any choice," replied Fulton, "unless he found a way to defeat my simulation, which I doubt. Even if he did, he's still going to want to unite his ship and get back to safety. Trust me, once I got the admiral to agree not to put Data on the saucer, our success was guaranteed."

Nechayev muttered through clenched teeth, "I wish we still hanged traitors like you. I would like to see you dangling from a yardarm!"

"Now, now, Admiral, show some grace in defeat. At least you can take solace in knowing that we'll finish the job Starfleet doesn't have the guts to do."

Riker yanked at the bindings around his wrists and ankles, but the tripolymer strands were too tough by far. He would slice through his own skin before breaking them. Suddenly, six shapes began to materialize on the bridge, and he stopped his struggling to watch the sparkling columns solidify into four humans and two Bajorans. All of them were carrying Klingon disruptor pistols, which gave him even more reason to cease his efforts at escape and remain calm.

The leader of the Maquis team was a young man with red hair and a bristling red mustache. Leveling his disruptor at the captives, he motioned to the others to take their places at the various stations on the bridge, then he nodded reverently to Fulton.

"Peacock," he said, "congratulations on a job well done."

"Thank you, Blue Moon."

"Childish tin soldiers," scoffed Nechayev, "with idiotic code names for each other."

"Silence!" snapped a hulking Bajoran male. He strode up the ramp and for a moment, it looked as though he might kick the defenseless woman in her stomach. She glared at him without flinching, the fire in her eyes burning more ferociously than ever.

"Don't injure them!" snapped the man called Blue Moon.

"Why?" growled the big Bajoran.

"Because those are our orders from the Architect." The man with the mustache bowed apologetically to Nechayev. "I'm sorry, Admiral, that won't happen again, unless you give us good cause. Our code names serve an important function because we don't want the Cardassians—or you—to know our true identities. Of course, those of us in the same cell know each other, but we have to protect those in other cells from Cardassian torture. I'm sure you can understand."

Nechayev twisted around, obviously still in pain. "I've fought Cardassians," she rasped, "but none of them are as underhanded as you people." The hulking Bajoran started toward her again, then changed his mind and went begrudgingly to his post.

"I'm sorry you feel that way," said Blue Moon. "I used to pilot a freighter among the colonies in the DMZ before it was the DMZ. I'm not saying the colonies were paradise, but there was a frontier spirit that anything was possible if you worked hard enough for it. Then the Cardassians—and the Federation—took that spirit away from us. I'm afraid, Admiral, you've given up the right to tell us what to do."

He strode down to the Conn and stood close enough to Riker that he could have lashed out with his feet and kicked him. Perhaps he could have brought the man down, but the sight of six disruptors and the beefy Bajoran glancing over his shoulder made the commander resist such foolhardiness. No, Riker and his crew had played the fool at every turn; now they would have to wait until they had a chance to do something intelligent.

The red-haired man tapped a Bajoran comm badge on his chest. "Blue Moon to *Shufola*. We are entering the cloud—proceed to your position. Maintain radio silence."

"Yes, sir," came the response.

Blue Moon leaned over the shoulder of the woman at the helm. "Take us to the center of the dust cloud at one-third impulse. Proceed with caution, because your instruments may give false readings. Everyone, watch for anomalies."

"What do you want me to do?" asked Henry Fulton.

The man walked over to Fulton and slapped him heartily on the back. "You've done enough. Just relax."

"But this is *my* operation," insisted Fulton.

Riker looked up with interest at this exchange, thinking that they might have found a chink in their captors' armor. Without the discipline of Starfleet, they all wanted to be in charge. How could they exploit this weakness? He caught Geordi looking at him and probably thinking the same thing.

Blue Moon looked tight-lipped under his mustache. "Peacock, no matter how important you were to the success of this operation, it isn't *your* operation. We all share the risks, the goals, and the rewards."

"But I was promised a ship . . ."

"Not *this* one," said the young man firmly. His expression softened. "In all honesty, I don't know what you were told when you were recruited. Our sympathizers in Starfleet have a very important job, but they are often unaware of the conditions out here on the front. I may be dead tomorrow, and so might you. But this ship has got a major duty to perform—to take out the Cardassian outpost at Spencerville."

"Spencerville?" croaked a voice. Everyone turned to see Admiral Nechayev struggling to crawl closer. "That's the largest colony we turned over to the Cardassians. It's full of families and children!"

The big Bajoran sneered. *"Cardassian* families and children."

Nechayev shook her head vehemently. "If a Galaxy-class starship destroys Spencerville, it will plunge us into war with Cardassia!"

Blue Moon nodded grimly. "We know. According to our intelligence, it's also the headquarters for the Cardassian death squads, which have been murdering our people all over the DMZ. We've been looking at Spencerville from the very beginning—as the symbol of what we lost—but we've never had the firepower to consider attacking it before. With this ship, we do. If that means bringing the Federation into the war, then so be it."

Even Henry Fulton seemed stunned by this revelation, and no one said another word until the helmswoman reported, "We're in the center of the cloud."

"Full stop," ordered the man code-named Blue Moon. "Send the distress signal."

Chapter Seven

ON THE HULL SECTION of the *Enterprise,* Data continued to scan the planet of Kitjef II for wreckage as Captain Picard alternated between pacing and gazing over his shoulder. Worf, Tate, and the other officers on the battle bridge searched for life signs, heat trails, vapor trails—anything that might be left from a disastrous reentry and crash—with negative results.

"I can't understand it," said the captain. "How do you lose a saucer that big."

Data twitched, not having an answer for the captain. "Shall I try a polar orbit, sir?"

"Would it do any good?" asked Picard. "They're not here, are they?"

"It would appear not," answered the android.

Actually he had reached that conclusion twelve point five minutes earlier, but it was not his position to call off the search. Besides, he had no alternative course of action to suggest to the captain.

Picard let out a frustrated sigh. "What do we do? Head back to Starbase 211 and tell them that we lost four senior officers and a saucer section? There's got to be some sign of them—they can't have vanished."

"Sir," said Worf in a puzzled voice, "I am receiving a distress signal. It appears to be a Galaxy-class starship."

"Where is it?"

The ridges on Worf's forehead compressed. "It's approximately seventeen light-years away, in the Thresher Dust Cloud."

"Seventeen light-years?" The captain shook his head. "Then it can't be the saucer section."

Data analyzed the signal on his own console and reached a conclusion within milliseconds. "On the contrary, sir, it *is* the saucer section. The signature matches exactly."

"That's impossible," said the captain. "How could they travel seventeen light-years without warp drive?"

"They could not," agreed Data, "under their own power. However, the saucer section could have been towed by a vessel with warp drive or could have been affected by some unknown anomaly. The signal is definitely coming from the Thresher Dust Cloud, seventeen light-years away. That region of space is known for causing sensor distortions and equipment malfunctions. We could be receiving some sort of subspace reflection, and the saucer might actually be elsewhere."

"Can we use long-range sensors?"

The android shook his head. "Sensors are ineffective in penetrating an ionized dust cloud. Only firsthand observation will confirm the source of the signal."

"Hail them, Mr. Worf."

"Hailing the distressed ship," said the Klingon. After a few moments, he shook his head. "They do not respond. It is possible our signals are not reaching them."

The captain frowned. "This couldn't be some sort of false reading left over from the simulation, could it?"

"No, sir," answered Data. "All systems are functioning within acceptable parameters."

Picard ran his hand over his skull. "Helm, set course for the Thresher Dust Cloud."

"Course laid in," answered Tate.

"One moment," said the captain. "Open a channel to Starbase 211. It's time we got some help. I also want my ship back in one piece."

"Yes, sir," answered Worf. After a minute, the Klingon reported, "I have Captain Slarn."

"On screen." Picard gritted his teeth as he faced the somber visage of the Vulcan commander of Starbase 211.

"Captain Picard," said Slarn, "I hope your mission has been a success."

"I wish it were," said Picard, "but we've run into some serious problems. The computer simulation turned out to be infected by a virus, and we were unable to gain control of our ship for almost two hours. During that time, the saucer section was supposed to have landed on Kitjef II, but instead it disappeared without a trace."

Slarn raised a white eyebrow. "That is unfortunate."

The captain shook his head at the profound understatement. "Yes, it is. Now we're receiving a distress signal from the Thresher Dust Cloud, which is closer to you than us, I believe. It could be the missing saucer."

"I am aware of the dust cloud," the Vulcan replied. "We advise ships to steer clear of it. The saucer could not have traveled there in such a short time."

"Unless it was towed," said Picard. "We don't know how it got there, but we have to check it out. How are repairs coming on *our* saucer section?"

"We are ahead of schedule," answered Slarn. "Repairs will be completed within the hour."

The captain nodded with satisfaction. "If that's the case, would it be possible to dispatch the saucer section to meet us at the dust cloud? We need to do a core dump to rid our computer of the virus, and the main computer on the *Enterprise* saucer is unaffected."

The Vulcan considered the question. "Normally, we would not release a vessel for active duty without extensive test flights."

"I know," said Picard, "but this is an emergency. Admiral Nechayev, Commander Riker, and two more senior officers are on that saucer section. There's a possibility of sabotage, although we don't know who's behind it."

The Vulcan nodded. "Very well. This will serve as the test flight. Do you have a captain in mind for the saucer section?"

"Both Dr. Crusher and Counselor Troi are qualified."

"I will speak with them immediately. Is there anything else, Captain?"

Picard shook his head. "No."

"Very well. Slarn out." His image blinked off the viewscreen.

The captain looked determinedly at his tiny crew on the battle bridge. "Helm, your course is set. Engage at maximum warp."

Bored. That was Deanna Troi as she wandered the staid, commercial wing of Starbase 211—a mixture of Federation government offices, consulates, entrepreneurs, money changers, and business services—all on a double-tiered pedestrian mall that tried unsuccessfully to look like a French Quarter, with fake brick and wrought iron. Once you got past the museums on Starbase 211, which she had done with unfortunate swiftness, there wasn't much of interest on the base. It was odd, but shore leave wasn't fun unless you had somebody to blow off steam with, and Deanna missed the people who were away on the mission.

Beverly Crusher had turned out to be good company in the museums, but she couldn't wait to actually lie around and do nothing. The doctor actually thought that R and R meant rest and relaxation, and she had a better accomplice for that in Guinan. Doing nothing was not something Deanna was able to accomplish with any sort of satisfaction—she longed for nightlife, dancing, a bit of excitement. But not with strangers. All the good dancers she knew were on that damn test flight.

If she hadn't paused on the second-story walkway to feel sorry for herself, Deanna might not have noticed the old-fashioned door with the antique knocker and large peephole. It was sandwiched between a travel agency and a store that sold security devices. The Betazoid touched the aged door, noting that it had a real brass doorknob that actually turned. She couldn't resist the sensation of the metal ball in her palm and the way it yielded to her touch—she had to turn it.

The peephole slapped open, and an eyeball peered down at her. "Who is it?" said a deep voice.

She straightened to attention like a schoolgirl caught in the teachers' lounge. "I just . . . I just wondered what this place was?"

"This is a private club," said the voice. "Look above the door."

Deanna gazed upward at a small but elegant plaque that simply carried the numeral 19.

"This is Club 19," the voice said arrogantly. "I take it you aren't a member?"

"No, I'm just passing through." She looked down at herself and realized that, except for her comm badge, she wasn't wearing anything that looked like a uniform—just her recreational clothes. "I'm Counselor Deanna Troi from the *Enterprise.*"

But the eyeball had been distracted away from the peephole, and the voice was talking to someone else. All she heard in the hushed tones were the words, "Yes, sir."

The eyeball returned. "Things are a bit slow today, and our membership chairman has graciously extended you a one-day complimentary membership. Won't you come in, Counselor Troi?"

The round doorknob turned from the other side, and the door swung open for her. Deanna strolled into a club that seemed to have come from a past century. Everything about it was old oak and cigars, even though no one was smoking. There were mirrors and old gas lamps and an ornate carved bar with crossed swords over the fireplace. For the adventuresome, there were card tables and a dartboard.

A dozen or so heads turned her way as she entered, and she spotted Andorian anteannae, floppy Ferengi earlobes, and handsome humans. The only women in the room were gathered in a dark corner, conversing among themselves. Several of the members rose politely to their feet, but first she wanted to thank the man who had opened the door. The majordomo was a tall, blue-skinned Bolian dressed in a tuxedo, and he seemed eminently above it all and bored with it at the same time.

"Welcome, Counselor Troi," he intoned with a bow. "I am Egot. Please call upon me if you require anything."

She smiled. "Thank you. May I ask you a question?"

"Please."

"How old are these furnishings? They're quite amazing."

The majordomo coughed, as if he was embarrassed to answer. "All of this is a holodeck. They could be sitting on a beach, cruising the galaxy on a space yacht, or lounging in a Roman bacchanal, but they seem to prefer this. Most peculiar."

He motioned farther into the inner sanctum. "Please make yourself comfortable. May I bring you a refreshment?"

"Tonic water with a twist of lime," she said, figuring that would go well in a place like this.

"As you wish." The Bolian bowed and shuffled away.

She was instantly intercepted by a middle-aged Ferengi, who was taller than the norm for his people. He was also dressed in expensive finery with several layers of latinum chains around his neck.

"Not *the* Counselor Troi of the *Enterprise?*" he gushed. "My, this is a privilege. My people speak highly of you—and of your mother! I have always gotten along well with Betazoids. My name is Plerbo, and I was wondering . . ."

He was cut off by a tall, blond-haired human who shoved his way into the conversation. "Hello,

Counselor Troi," he said with a charming drawl, "mah name is Burt Peters, and I was wondering if you would like to join me for a drink?"

"But we were playing poker," protested the Ferengi.

"Poker?" asked Deanna with interest.

"Do you play, ma'am?" asked Burt Peters.

Deanna tried to remember what Will Riker had always told her about playing poker with strangers—act as if you knew nothing.

"I've seen my uncle play a few times," she answered. "I always wanted to try it."

"Gambling is strictly forbidden on a starbase," said the handsome blond man, "so we play for personal favors. A personal favor might be a payment-free loan of ten bars of gold-pressed latinum, for example."

The Ferengi leered at her, and a drop of drool formed where one of his teeth protruded over his lower lip. "Or a personal favor could be an actual *personal* favor. I think you get my drift."

Deanna Troi batted her dark eyes at him and answered in a low voice, "Yes, I get your drift. I don't suppose one little hand of poker would hurt me any."

"Right this way," said the man with the southern drawl, not hiding his amusement. They arrived at a card table in the far corner of the room, where a young Klingon sat, shuffling the cards with impatience. Upon seeing Deanna Troi, his glower changed to a look of suspicion. "I thought we were going to play *poker*," he grumbled.

"We are!" answered the Ferengi with a warning glare. "This is Counselor Troi of the starship *Enterprise,* and she's agreed to sit in for a hand or two."

The Klingon crossed his beefy arms and glowered at the intruder. "My mother told me never to play cards with a Betazoid." He grinned. "But I would like to watch."

"Watch then," she said, taking a seat, "if you haven't got the courage to play."

The Klingon frowned at her and growled, "Count me in! One hand. What are the stakes?"

"Let us see our hands, no draw, and then we'll bet accordingly," said Deanna. "Isn't that called stud poker?"

"Yes," said Burt Peters, brushing back his long blond hair. "Why don't you deal, little lady."

Deanna wasted no time in shuffling, getting a cut from the Klingon, and dealing five cards to each of the four players. She pretended to study her own cards, but in truth she was watching the other players. The Betazoid had no intentions of using her empathic abilities, which wouldn't work on the Ferengi anyway, but she could use the powers of observation available to any poker player. She could study their body language, expressions, and posture.

From his slumped shoulders, Burt Peters was definitely disappointed with his hand, but he was growing more optimistic as he thought about it. He probably had nothing but one high card—an ace or a king—and was thinking that the odds were good for a high card to win at a game of no-draw stud.

Across from her, the Ferengi maintained a total poker face, and Deanna wondered if a good hand might have sparked at least a gleam of greed in his eyes. He would play a mediocre hand shrewdly, unless she distracted him. The Klingon glowered suspiciously at her, and she assumed it would be a battle to keep him from folding.

Deanna glanced at her own cards, trying to look puzzled. In reality, her pair of nines was probably a winner.

"I'll bet first," she said cheerfully. "But I don't have much money."

"A personal favor is always welcome," the Ferengi reminded her.

She placed her bet and turned to the blond man. "That's my bet. Are you in?"

He grinned back at her. "Counselor Troi, how long are you going to be on base?"

"Several more days at least. The *Enterprise* is undergoing repairs, and much of the crew bridge is gone."

"Very well," said the handsome southerner, "I'll bet a dinner at the restaurant of your choice."

"No thank you," she said politely, "how about some currency, and the winner can buy himself dinner."

"All right," growled the human, "a no-payment loan of a strip of gold-pressed latinum." To seal the bet, he took a disposable padd from a pouch on his waist, entered some figures, and tossed it on the table.

The Ferengi took off his latinum necklaces and

dropped them on the table. "How about a perpetu-
al loan of my necklaces?"

"Fine with me," answered Deanna in a teasing
voice.

Now it was up to the Klingon, and his scowl
deepened as he looked at the loot on the table, then
at the attractive Betazoid, then at his cards.

"Are you in or out?" Deanna asked.

"I think I will listen to my mother." He tossed
his cards facedown on the table.

"All right," said Deanna. She spread her cards
on the table and looked forlornly at the two nines.
"That one pair is all I have. What about you
gentlemen?"

The human scowled and threw his cards on the
table. The Ferengi tossed down his cards and
claimed, "I've got a pair of fours, and that beats
nines if they're both red!"

"I don't think so," said Deanna with a smile,
hauling in the necklaces and the padd with the
promissory note. Her comm badge beeped. "I
wonder what that is?"

She tapped the badge and answered, "Troi
here."

"This is Captain Slarn, station commander,"
said an efficient voice. "There's been an emergency, and you may have to join the *Enterprise* saucer
section on a mission. Can you report to docking
bay 27 as soon as possible?"

"Yes, sir," she snapped, "on my way." She rose
quickly from the table and stuffed the loot in her
bag. "If that fellow ever gets back with my drink,

one of you can have it. It's been a pleasure. Good-
bye, gentlemen."

As she gracefully exited, the Ferengi shook his
head. "She just missed one hell of a personal
favor."

Beverly Crusher eased her naked body in the
creamy slime, keeping one hand dry to check that
her auburn hair was still pinned high upon
her head. Chilly at first, the lashnut milk adjusted instantly to her body temperature and
flowed all around her luxuriously. She sighed and
submerged in the liquid up to her chin, floating
on the buoyant silkiness. The small pool took on a
mother-of-pearl appearance with shiny swirls of
gray, blue, white, and gold, depending upon the
thermal currents. For a day and a half, Beverly
and Guinan had been on a waiting list for the
lashnut treatment, and now they were alone in the
rippling pool, surrounded by dark mirrors with
tiny lights dancing behind them. It had been worth
the wait.

Guinan was just taking off her robe, having
needed a few extra minutes to stuff her thick hair
into a bathing cap. "Does it feel as good as it
smells?" asked the dark-skinned El-Aurian.

With all the sensory delights of the lashnut milk,
Beverly had hardly noticed the fresh, citruslike
smell. "Yes," she breathed.

Beverly closed her eyes and didn't know that
Guinan had entered the pool until the creamy milk
sloshed against her cheek.

"Ooooh," moaned Guinan, sinking all the way to her lower lip. "Now I know where I'm spending the rest of the week."

"Yes," agreed Beverly, "nothing could get me out of here."

"Not even if the captain came back early?"

Beverly smiled. "That might be tempting, but I see Jean-Luc everyday. We don't have *this* on the *Enterprise*."

"Good thing," replied Guinan, "or we'd never get any work done." She ran her fingers through the pearly liquid. "It's like floating in egg whites."

"But better for your skin," said the doctor. She closed her eyes again and tried to imagine herself floating in a lagoon on some tropical isle. It was that kind of feeling, warm and comforting, like being back in the womb. She brushed a strand of hair off her forehead, and a bit of the liquid seeped into her eye. It didn't sting; in fact, it felt as soothing as a teardrop. This lashnut milk was truly amazing stuff.

"Why *don't* we have this on the *Enterprise?*" she asked rhetorically. "You know, we're going to look years younger when we get out."

"Good. I could stand to lose a century or two." Guinan stretched out her arms and let them float on the creamy waves. "I haven't felt so good since I was in the . . ." She stopped suddenly.

"In the what?"

"Just a place," said the long-lived El-Aurian. "A place that I never expect to see again."

Beverly didn't press for information. The bartender of the Ten-Forward lounge had a mysterious past, one that only Jean-Luc had any knowledge of. There was no point asking her questions because Guinan was a wonderful listener but not a great talker. Besides, Beverly's brain was beginning to feel as mushy and insubstantial as the filmy substance that flowed around her. Even if Guinan wanted to talk, she didn't think she'd be capable of holding an intelligent conversation. She listened to the echo of swirling milk and watched the tiny lights twinkle distantly within the smoky mirrors.

As her body became more disconnected from her mind, Beverly pictured Jean-Luc Picard joining her. Indeed, she did wish that he would return quickly to the starbase, not to keep her company but to partake in a shore leave that he needed as much as anyone. Life had a way of being grossly unfair, she decided. It wasn't his fault that the bridge had been damaged, and he shouldn't be punished by missing out on the only shore leave he was likely to get for months. She hated to place blame, but Admiral Nechayev deserved the brunt of it. Jean-Luc was much too fine an officer to have an admiral gunning for him.

There were times when Beverly wondered what it would be like to command a vessel like the *Enterprise* on a permanent basis. It couldn't be any more work than being the chief medical officer, and it offered substantially more prestige. Nevertheless, whenever she thought seriously about a career change to the command ranks, something like this saucer mission came up and convinced her that she should stay where she was. Beverly didn't think she could put up with Admiral Nechayev for more than ten minutes without telling her off. Doctors were allowed to voice their opinions to anybody in Starfleet—so long as their comments had a medical basis. Command officers could not do that. No, the doctor finally decided, she didn't want Jean-Luc's job.

She was startled by a knock on the mirrored door that shut them off from the rest of the universe.

"Who's there?" asked Guinan grumpily.

"Captain Slarn, commander of the base."

Guinan looked at Beverly and wrinkled her nose. "They want to get us out—we're having too much fun."

"I know *I* am," agreed Beverly. "What is it, Captain? We're rather indisposed at the moment."

"I assure you," said the brusque voice, "I would not interrupt your recreation if it were not an emergency."

Beverly thought about grabbing her robe, but the lashnut milk was fairly opaque. Besides, she was certain that the Vulcan would have very little interest in ogling two naked women.

"Enter!" she called.

A doorway within the mirrors slid open, and the venerable Vulcan strode into the chamber. Unlike a human male, who would have looked away out of embarrassment, Slarn regarded them as if they had been fully clothed and sitting in his office.

"I do apologize for the interruption," he began, "but there's been a problem with the saucer mission."

Beverly nearly bolted upright, and then she remembered her state of undress. "What happened?"

"As far as we know no one has been injured, but the saucer section reportedly disappeared during the simulated attack."

"Disappeared?" asked Guinan. "How do you lose a saucer section?"

The Vulcan cocked his head. "That is the question of the hour. I have little information beyond what I have given you, only that Admiral Nechayev, Commander Riker, and two more senior officers are missing with the craft. In approximately 30 minutes, we will finish our repairs on the *Enterprise*'s saucer section, and Captain Picard has requested that someone pilot the saucer to a rendezvous at the Thresher Dust Cloud. You can see it with the naked eye from here—it is about fourteen hours away at full impulse. Captain Picard believes the missing saucer section is there, although that is possible only if it were towed by a vessel with warp drive."

"If I've learned anything from working in space," said Beverly, "it's that *nothing* is impossible."

Slarn nodded as if he agreed. "Then you will command the saucer section?"

"Yes. I'll be at the dock as soon as I get dressed."

"Very well," answered the Vulcan. "Counselor Troi has already been informed, as she was easier to locate. I will stress to our repair crew the need to finish quickly. I must warn you, without proper test flights, I cannot absolutely guarantee the reliability of the new bridge module."

"I'm sure you've done a great job," said Beverly.

"I believe that our repairs have been satisfactory." With that, he turned and marched out.

Beverly sighed. "I guess my shore leave is going to be cut short, too."

"You're not going alone, are you?"

"Well, he mentioned something about Deanna Troi." Beverly emerged from the mother-of-pearl pool, grabbed her robe, and slipped it around her slim torso. "I would prefer to take as few of the regular crew as possible, because I know how much they need this shore leave."

She laughed at the irony. "Now I'm in the same position Jean-Luc was in, as I decide to take the minimum number of people."

"I'm going with you," declared Guinan. She slid out of the swirling liquid and clutched her own robe. At Beverly's quizzical expression, she shrugged and said, "I don't want to see you and Deanna all alone out there. You might need a morale officer."

"How about science officer?" asked Beverly. "If you can coax a chocolate milkshake out of a food slot, you can work a science console."

Guinan smiled. "If it's all the same to you, I'd just as soon stick with 'morale officer.'"

They showered and dressed as quickly as possible.

Crusher contacted more bridge officers, Mason and Gherink, and asked nicely if they would volunteer for the extracurricular mission, giving up their shore leave in the process. They agreed, of course. As ship's doctor, she wanted as many of the crew as possible to continue their shore leave, so she made certain that no one but her tiny band knew about the emergency. If the others found out, hundreds of them would come running to volunteer.

She and Guinan strode through the terminal, hardly noticing the dazzling laser show over their heads or the milling passengers. Outside bay 27, they were met by Mason and Gherink, a human male and a female Deltan, respectively. The party of four marched through the airlock, up the extendable docking port, and into the turbolift. They emerged from the lift onto the main bridge of the *Enterprise,* bereft of its hull section, and Beverly noticed the four dimunitive Bynars who were bouncing from one console to another, checking last-minute diagnostics, she presumed.

The bridge looked exactly as before. Beverly's attention was directed toward the command chair, where Deanna Troi sat.

The Betazoid got to her feet and faced Beverly. "I was ordered to report to the bridge—I assumed that you would report to sickbay," said the empath. Deanna was wearing a proper uniform, showing her rank of commander.

The doctor clasped her hands in front of her. "I see. Well, I was also told to report to the bridge— do we have a fight over who commands this ship, or does one of us volunteer to be first officer?"

Deanna thought for a moment. "You've had more experience. I volunteer to be first officer."

Beverly nodded appreciatively. "I couldn't ask for better. Take the Tactical station. Mason on Conn. Gherink on Science."

The acting captain strode to the command chair, sat down, and stared at the Bynars. "Excuse me," she said loudly, "how long is it going to be until these repairs are finished?"

In unison, two of the pale, fidgety Bynars stopped their work and turned toward her. "Approximately fifteen . . ."

"Minutes," finished the other.

"I enjoyed your concert the other night," said Beverly. "Weren't the two of you in it?"

"We were," answered one.

"Thank you," said the other.

Beverly nodded pleasantly. "You have five minutes to finish up and get out of here."

"That is . . ." began one.

"Not enough time," replied the other.

"Then perhaps you would like to come with us. We have a long way to go, and we don't have warp drive. So we want to get started as soon as possible."

"This is . . ."

"Highly irregular."

"You can take that up with Captain Slarn," said Beverly. "You now have four and a half minutes."

The Bynars returned to their frenzied activity, and Beverly leaned back in the command chair. "Troi, request permission to cast off. Helm, set course for the Thresher Dust Cloud, and Science, please help Mr. Mason locate the dust cloud."

"I'm bringing it up," said Gherink, furiously punching commands on her console. "It looks like it's nearby."

"Course laid in," reported Lieutenant Mason.

Beverly shifted in her chair. "Ops, what is our approximate arrival time at the dust cloud?"

"Fourteen point two hours," answered the Delosian.

"Then we'd better get started. Is the repair crew about done?"

One of the Bynars whirled around. "We cannot guarantee . . ."

"Reliability," said his partner.

Beverly shrugged. "Thank you for your concern, but I don't really believe in guarantees, anyway. My report will note that you warned us."

All four Bynars looked at one another, then scuttled off the bridge and into the turbolift. Beverly nodded with satisfaction, then said, "Computer, place all command functions under Dr. Beverly Crusher, authorization Crusher Omega three."

"Commands transferred," answered the computer. Beverly didn't know why she expected to hear a different computer voice on a newly installed bridge, but it was the same voice they had been hearing for years.

"The Bynars have just left the ship," said the strapping Delosian female on the Ops console. "Closing airlocks."

"We are cleared for departure," announced Deanna Troi.

Beverly rose to her feet and nodded at the Ops station. "Cast off."

"Yes, sir."

They heard the sounds of the docking latches

and ports retracting, then the deck tilted slightly under their feet.

"We are under way," reported Gherink. "All systems normal."

"Helm," said Beverly, crossing her arms, "full speed to the Thresher Dust Cloud."

Chapter Eight

THE NERVE ENDINGS in Riker's left leg were screaming in that weird sensation of pain and prickling that comes when the circulation is restricted for too long. With difficulty, he twisted around on the bridge of the prototype saucer and saw that Geordi and Admiral Nechayev were in equally miserable condition. The commander gazed up at the main viewscreen at the same thing they had been staring at for the better of an hour—dense, swirling dust clouds of a metallic magenta color. He had no idea how long they would be waiting for the next act of this bizarre drama.

The Maquis personnel at the critical stations were paying very little attention to their captors, but Fulton and the man with the red mustache occasionally glanced their way. Riker hated to ask these people for favors, but they couldn't remain trussed up like this for long without risking serious nerve damage. Seeing Nechayev's ashen expression, he was worried that the admiral was suffering from the brutal kick to the stomach she had received. He had to do something to alleviate their pain.

"Captain?" he asked in a hoarse voice.

Both Fulton and the man known as Blue Moon whirled around to look at him. "Yes?" asked the red-haired man, stepping forward.

Riker wanted to make small talk—to show them he wasn't a demon—but the prickly sensations in his leg made him rush to the point. "Captain, we're in pain. Do we have to stay tied up like this?"

"Yes," snapped Fulton. "We don't have a brig on this saucer."

"You've got six disruptors and an empty ready room right there." Riker nodded his head toward the closed door just beyond the Ops console. "Please."

Blue Moon walked to the ready room door, which opened at his approach, and glanced inside. "I don't see how they could escape from here. Fulton, I'll cover you while you cut their bindings."

"I think you're making a mistake," said the turncoat, refusing to budge.

"Then you cover me while I untie them." The young man handed Fulton his disruptor pistol, then reached into his boot and pulled out a stiletto.

He crossed to Geordi, who was closest to him, and cut his bindings with swift flicks of his knife.

Relief spread over the engineer's face as he sat up and rubbed his wrists. "Thank you."

As Fulton looked on with disapproval and a leveled disruptor, Blue Moon performed the same task for Riker and Nechayev. The admiral, with her sandy hair plastered to her forehead, sat up and glared at him, not revealing the slightest hint of thanks or relief. Riker sat up and massaged his leg; after a few moments, normal feeling began to return.

"I'll remember your kindness," he said.

The young man returned his knife to the hidden sheath in his boot. "We Maquis are not cruel—we only do the things we have to do in order to win back what is ours."

"And that includes wiping out hundreds of families at Spencerville?" asked Nechayev with disdain.

Blue Moon turned to her. "Do you know what the Cardassians call Spencerville now that they've taken it over? *Elo-menkiar.* Roughly that translates into 'blood of the fools.' That's what they think of us, Admiral, that we're fools and cowards, fit only to be stomped under their boots."

"Well, do you have to prove they're right?" asked Nechayev, rubbing her ankles. "It's easy to make war—far more difficult to make peace. Only fools start wars they can't finish."

The big Bajoran whirled around and glared at the admiral. "If you don't stick her in that room, I'm going to shut her up for good."

The young man nodded in agreement and took his disruptor back from Fulton. "All right, get in the ready room."

Battling his aching muscles, Riker staggered to his feet. He moved to help the admiral up, but a Maquis female waved him back with her disruptor. He waited until Nechayev and Geordi managed to get to their feet unaided, then he led the way toward the captain's ready room. With half a dozen weapons trained on them, they limped into the small office and waited as the door shut behind them.

Nechayev finally held her stomach and showed some of the anguish she was suffering. "Thank you, Commander."

"Are you all right?" asked Geordi.

"I'm still alive," she rasped. She lowered her voice. "Now, what's the plan for escape?"

Riker smiled despite the dire circumstances. In a fight, he wanted Alynna Nechayev on his side. He motioned around their stark cell. "The vents are too small to crawl through, and there's only that one door. I mainly wanted to give us a chance to recover and talk."

Geordi went to one of the walls and began to feel up and down the panel with his hands.

Riker joined him and rapped on the wall. It sounded fairly hollow. "How thick is this paneling?"

Geordi shrugged. "If we had tools or a phaser, it wouldn't be much problem to break through."

"We've got our fists and our feet," said Nechayev with determination. She gave Riker an appraising glance. "You're big enough to kick through that wall."

"That may not be necessary, admiral," Geordi said quickly. Riker made a mental note to thank the engineer for saving him from having to formulate a tactful reply for Nechayev.

"I'm listening," she said skeptically.

"Well, normally there's at least one panel on this side of the room. And, unless I'm mistaken, there's a large cavity behind it that leads to energy conduits and a Jeffries tube." Geordi continued tapping the wall until suddenly his face lit up with a triumphant smile. "Admiral, Commander, it looks like our luck is about to change." The panel creaked loudly as Geordi began to pull on it.

"It can't be helped, Mister La Forge," the admiral whispered. "Can we keep the door shut for a few seconds?"

Geordi pointed to a membrane keypad on the wall near the door. "If somebody leaned on the door control, they could keep the door shut. For a while."

Nechayev nodded and limped to the door. Her hand poised over the keypad. "Ready when you are."

Riker took a deep breath. He wanted to tell the admiral that the chances of all three of them escaping from this room before the Maquis blasted through the door with their disruptors were very slim. Hell, the chances of *one* of them escaping were slim. The admiral already knew the risks, he was sure.

"You go through first," he told Geordi. "Traveling through the dark is no problem for you. If we get separated, meet in transporter room three."

"Yes, sir," said the chief engineer, his shoulders tensing as he continued pulling. "Damn, it's stuck," he said.

"My turn," replied Riker as he began kicking at the panel to open the passage completely.

Riker turned to Admiral Nechayev and nodded. Her hand hit the keypad at the same moment that his first kick dented the panel. Geordi gave it another kick, and the two of them were soon making enough noise to alert all the Maquis in the galaxy. At once, there were angry shouts on the other side of the door, plus kicking and banging that rivaled their own.

"Back! Stand back!" they heard someone yell.

Panting, with sweat running down his face, Riker turned to see a black hole burning in the center of the door. Another hole began to burn a few centimeters away, then another one near the edge— until it looked as if the entire door was aflame! Nechayev covered her eyes and shrank back from the sparks and melting debris, but she never took her hand off the door control.

"Hurry!" she shouted.

Geordi and Riker redoubled their efforts at opening the panel, and it finally began to buckle. With his VISOR, Geordi could see the cavity he expected just beyond the mangled wall, along with energy conduits for the food replicator that should have been there. He also smelled the acrid smoke from the burning door, and he turned to see a disruptor beam blast through and take out a chunk of the wall opposite the door. Nechayev fell to the floor and crawled away from a shower of sparks.

With brute force, Riker grabbed the remainder of the panel and heaved it away from the wall, opening a slit about twenty centimeters wide.

"Move it!" he shouted at Geordi, groaning to hold the escape route open.

Before Geordi could squeeze through, there was a terrible sound as the beefy Bajoran crashed through the burning door, blasting cinders everywhere. The sight of him leveling his disruptor was enough to get Geordi scurrying through the narrow slit. His last glimpse of the ready room was the sight of Riker whirling around and smashing the Bajoran in the mouth. The two big men tumbled to the floor as more Maquis piled into the burning room.

Luckily, the thick smoke covered Geordi's escape, yet he was able to see perfectly well with his VISOR. He heard angry shouts as Riker and Nechayev put up a valiant fight behind him, and he felt momentarily guilty about his escape. Then a disruptor beam streaked by just centimeters over his head and blasted out a section of electrical tubing. He crawled on all fours down the narrow access tunnel, hoping he could reach the Jeffries tube before the indiscriminate fire reached him. Even in total darkness, he could see the opening in the floor just a few meters away. As another disruptor beam scorched the tunnel, he flopped to his stomach and dove headfirst into the Jeffries tube.

Geordi caught the top rung of the ladder with his hands and curled into a ball, doing a flip that left him dangling in a vertical tube that plummeted a hundred meters straight down. He dropped rung after rung, letting his arms do most of the work and only intermittently touching the ladder with his feet. Angry voices echoed above him, and he knew they were coming after him. They would be shooting down the narrow tube in a few seconds, with a very good chance of picking him off, so he swung his body into a horizontal tube only two decks below the bridge. He pulled his head out of the Jeffries tube just as a disruptor beam shattered the ladder.

He crawled on all fours trying to put distance between himself and his pursuers, not really knowing where he was going. He needed a plan, but what? Riker had said to meet in transporter room three, but he didn't think the commander was going to make his appointment. Riker had helped him escape; now it was time to return the favor. With grim determination on his face, Geordi took a turn in the access tunnel and headed for the nearest transporter room.

As he crawled, he took stock of the situation. There were only seven Maquis, counting Fulton. They had all the weapons, but the saucer was an awfully large ship to search, especially when they were searching for a man who knew every tunnel and tube like the inside of his VISOR. The Maquis probably had dozens of reinforcements on their other ship, but they couldn't use the transporters to beam them over, not inside this dust cloud.

However, the transporters should still work *with-*

in the ship. Geordi hoped the Maquis wouldn't figure that out for a few minutes, at least.

They hadn't said it in so many words, but he was certain that the Maquis planned to use the saucer as a Trojan horse, luring Picard and the hull section into the dust cloud. As the captain wouldn't be able to use his transporters, sensors, or tractor beam inside the cloud, he would be forced to dock in order to find out what was happening. After docking with the saucer, Picard and his small crew would be ambushed and the entire ship would belong to the Maquis.

Geordi had to keep that from happening.

"Where did La Forge go?" demanded Henry Fulton, who was standing behind the Bajoran interrogating Riker.

Riker tried to talk, but he had a split lower lip from the escape attempt. "I don't know," he mumbled. "We didn't have time to discuss it."

The Bajoran drew his fist back. "Should I hit him?"

"Go ahead, play rough," said Riker. "You people deserve to live with Cardassians." Fulton and the Bajoran sneered in unison.

Groggily, Riker looked over at Admiral Nechayev, who was tied up to another chair on the bridge. She was being interrogated, although not beaten up, by the man with the red mustache. She glared at him defiantly, her lips tightly sealed. When she looked over at Riker, she gave him an encouraging smile. They could pummel that woman all day, figured Riker, and not get so much as a word, except for a good bawling out.

Fulton finally broke first. "We'll just have to go look for him."

"With seven people?" asked the red-haired man. "Where would you start first?"

The Bajoran grabbed Riker by his torn collar and shook him. "This one knows. Let me work on him."

Riker braced himself as the big man let go of his collar and drew back a beefy fist. But just as his assailant was about to wallop him, Riker felt a curious tingling in his body, and he saw the Bajoran's expression change from one of cruel confidence to utter confusion. Desperately, the Bajoran swung at Riker's head, but his fist sailed harmlessly through empty air.

The commander materialized in a clump in the center of a transporter platform, and he saw Geordi rushing to pick him up.

"No!" he groaned. "Get the admiral!"

Geordi ran back to the transporter console and furiously worked the controls. Riker twisted away to make room for the admiral, whom he expected to materialize on the transporter pad beside him. Seconds later, only her comm badge appeared, with a scrap of her uniform still clinging to it.

"Damn it, only one pad was active," muttered Geordi. "There wasn't enough power to bring you both here at once, and now they've figured out that I got the coordinates from your comm badge." The engineer rushed to Riker's side and began to untie him. "They'll be here any second. You look terrible."

"Thanks," mumbled Riker. He staggering to his feet and gingerly touched his swollen face. "I mean, thanks for rescuing me."

Geordi yanked his own comm badge off his tunic and tossed it onto the transporter platform next to Nechayev's. "Better lose our comm badges, or they'll use them to trace us."

"Right." Riker took off his own badge and dropped it on the deck. They dashed to the door of the transporter room and peered cautiously down the corridor. Seeing no one, they were soon jogging along the deserted walkway.

LaForge suddenly held out his hand and pushed Riker against the bulkhead. Holding perfectly still, they heard footsteps pounding down the corridor behind them. Riker tapped a panel near the closest door, which slid open, and they ducked inside an empty storage room. As the door shut behind them, they held their breath, waiting for the footsteps to thunder past.

After the corridor was silent again, Geordi let out his breath. "Thank God this saucer isn't fully equipped. We'd be in trouble if it had a tricorder in every locker like the *Enterprise*."

"All right, how can we warn the captain not to dock?"

Geordi frowned in thought. "I'm assuming they sent out a standard, class-one distress signal. If we could convert that signal to a class three, which also warns of danger, we could get the point across without alerting the Maquis. We need to get to the subspace transceiver on deck five."

"Let's go," said Riker. Bracing himself for a disruptor blast, he opened the door, but the corridor was empty. "If either one of us doesn't make it, the other one has to get through."

"Understood," said Geordi grimly.

Without another word, they set out at a dead run down the corridor.

"Coming out of warp drive," reported Data from the Ops station. "The Thresher Dust Cloud is two thousand kilometers dead ahead."

That last bit of information was unnecessary, thought Picard, as the magenta dust cloud completely filled every viewscreen on the battle bridge. They had reached their destination, the source of the distress signal, but the saucer was completely invisible inside the vast cloud.

"Sensor readings?" asked Picard.

The android shook his head. "Sensor readings are unreliable inside the dust cloud. Actually I am showing *two* ships, but I am unable to get a clear reading on either one of them. It is possible that one is a reflection of the other."

"Two ships?" asked Picard. "Try hailing them, Mr. Worf."

"Hailing frequencies open," said the Klingon. After a moment, he shook his head. "There is no response. However, the distress signal is very strong here. This is the source."

Data turned to look at the captain. "To be

certain, we must enter the cloud and conduct firsthand observations."

"Very well," said the captain. "Shields up."

"Shields up," echoed Worf.

With a nod, Picard ordered, "Helm, proceed with caution at one-third impulse, dead reckoning."

The Maquis female on the Tactical station of the saucer section suddenly bolted upright. "They're here!" she gasped. "They just tried to hail us!"

Timothy Wiley, also known as Blue Moon, shifted in the command chair. "You're sure it's the hull section?"

"Who else could it be?" sneered Henry Fulton.

Wiley bounced to his feet. "Kill running lights. I want us to look dead in space. Any word on the two escapees?"

"No," grumbled the beefy Bajoran. "Do you want to recall our search team?"

"Wait a minute," said Henry Fulton, limping toward the command chair and confronting the freighter pilot. "Blue Moon, you put this entire operation at risk with your softhearted pity. You're not tough enough for this job. *I'm* taking over this ship and this operation."

Wiley looked around at his fellow Maquis for some support, but all of them, including the Bajoran, turned pointedly away. Well, he thought, the Maquis wasn't Starfleet, or even a well-run commercial venture. Once your crew lost faith in you, there was no way to force them to follow you.

With one mistake, he had lost their faith and the command of a Galaxy-class starship. There was no point in arguing or crying about it—the success of the mission was still the most important thing.

He motioned toward the command chair and stepped back. "It's all yours, Peacock."

"May the Prophets guide you," the Bajoran told the new captain.

With a wide grin, Fulton planted himself in the command chair and handed his weapon to Wiley. "Keep the admiral covered, if you think you're up to it."

The young man smoothed back his mustache. "Peacock, someday you may need to beg someone for mercy. I hope *you're* up to it."

"Dim bridge lights and running lights," ordered Fulton, ignoring him. "Recall the search team—we need to prepare our ambush. Riker and La Forge are in hiding and haven't got any weapons, so I don't see how much trouble they can cause."

"Aye, sir." The Bajoran tapped his comm badge. "Search party, return to the bridge immediately."

"If they're still in the simulation," said Fulton, "they'll dock quickly. If somehow they beat it, they may take a few minutes to decide, but it's still their only option. I hope our other ship is ready."

"They have just entered the dust cloud," reported the Maquis officer on Ops.

Fulton rubbed his hands together and leaned forward excitedly. "On screen!"

The Ops officer adjusted the main viewer, and they saw the twin nacelles emerge from one cloud and slip into another, looking like some ghostly reflection. The hull section abruptly changed course and dipped underneath the saucer section. The Ops officer quickly adjusted the view, and they watched the hull section rise slowly toward them. It looked like a hawk riding the wind against a black-and-magenta sky.

"They've gone into docking approach!" shouted Fulton ecstatically.

There were cheers all around the bridge, except for Admiral Nechayev, who said somberly, "Commander Fulton, it's not too late for you to stop this madness."

Fulton waggled his thumb at his former superior. "If she speaks again, kill her."

Timothy Wiley looked forlornly at the feisty admiral, remembering the words of the Architect, who had ordered him not to harm any Starfleet personnel. But the Architect wasn't here, and Wiley wasn't in charge anymore.

"Just be quiet," he whispered to her, "and I'll do what I can to see that you're released."

"Right," she scoffed. "I know too much about all of you. You'll kill me."

Fulton whirled around and glared at the two of them. "Blue Moon, I gave you an order."

"Which I am respectfully disobeying," answered Timothy Wiley, his spine erect. "She can't do us any harm, and we might need her. She's a valuable hostage, if nothing else."

The five other Maquis members watched tensely, waiting to see how this power struggle would play out. Fulton glowered at them and said, "I'll deal with both of you later. Right now, I've got a starship to capture."

"The hull section is still in docking approach," said the Ops officer.

Wiley let out a sigh, knowing that he had only put off the inevitable. In all likelihood, Admiral Nechayev would die before this day was over, and so would a dozen other Starfleet officers, despite his best intentions. These were the first Starfleet officers he had personally encountered since joining the Maquis, and they were not the arrogant lackeys he had been led to believe they were. They were human beings with an acute sense of pride, duty, and loyalty. He envied their discipline and chain of command; he was weary of fighting for the right to do his job. For the first time, Timothy Wiley began to have doubts about the methods and goals of the Maquis.

Why should anyone help them fight Cardassians if they acted just like Cardassians?

Fulton rose from the command chair and limped toward the main viewscreen. Majestically, the hull section rose toward them, its dorsal breaking through the magenta clouds.

"Beautiful, isn't it?" said Henry Fulton with pride. "It reminds me of a poem—the one about the spider and the fly."

Captain Picard watched the underbelly of the saucer section as it loomed ever closer on his viewscreen. He wished there was a better way to check the status of the saucer other than docking with it, but there wasn't. If he didn't perform this task, then somebody else would have to, and it was clearly his responsibility. Nevertheless, the question of how the saucer section had ended up here—without warp drive—still haunted him. Only the fact that he had seen more than his share of inexplicable phenomena in space allowed him to proceed without undue hesitation.

"Lower shields," said Picard.

"Shields lowered," replied Worf.

"Data," said the captain, "will the dust cloud affect the docking procedure?"

"It will have some effect on the tractor beams," answered the android, "but I can compensate manually."

Picard nodded. "Assume manual control at your discretion." As an afterthought, he added, "Is there any sign of that second ship?"

"Yes, sir. I have a clearer sensor signal, and it appears to be a freighter of some sort. Perhaps whatever anomaly brought the saucer section to this location also brought the freighter here."

"As soon as we dock," said Picard, "we'll send a shuttlecraft to investigate. Estimated time to docking?"

"Fifty-five seconds," answered the android. "I have assumed manual control."

"Proceed with caution," said the captain. He had a bad feeling, a feeling honed from twenty-seven years of command, but he couldn't put it into words. Besides, if docking was the only way to get the saucer section out of this infernal dust cloud, then he had to do it.

"Twenty seconds until docking," reported Data. "Firing thrusters, extending grab plates."

The captain took a deep breath and watched as the underbelly of the saucer completely filled his viewscreen. If he'd been standing on top of the hull section, he'd almost be close enough to reach out and touch the saucer.

"Sir!" said Worf with concern. "The distress signal has changed. It is now a class-*three* signal."

"Abort docking," ordered Picard. "All stop."

Data instantly entered the command at his console. "Docking aborted."

Captain Picard turned to look at his security officer. "Are you sure, Lieutenant?"

"Yes, sir," answered the Klingon. "We are receiving a distress signal with a warning of unspecified danger."

"Could it be a distortion caused by the dust cloud?"

Worf shook his head. "No, sir, not at this range."

"I have verified the change in distress classification," said Data. "Perhaps they are injured."

Picard scowled and stepped closer to Ensign Tate at the Conn. "Reverse course to a distance of five thousand kilometers, half impulse."

"Yes, sir," answered the ensign, entering the change of course.

With a mixture of relief and frustration, Picard watched the saucer section recede into the distance. "What is going on here? Hail them again, Mr. Worf, and keep hailing them until they answer."

"Yes, sir."

* * *

On the main bridge, the big Bajoran stared in horror at the viewscreen. "They're retreating!"

"They're also hailing us again," muttered the woman on Tactical.

Henry Fulton bolted to his feet. "What the hell are they doing? What's happening?"

The Tactical officer shook her head. "They want to know why we changed our distress signal!"

Several meters away, Timothy Wiley looked down at Admiral Nechayev and saw a broad smile on her bruised face.

"So you think that letting two Starfleet officers run free will have no effect," she said with amusement. "I'm glad you people are such idiots."

Fulton made a threatening move toward the admiral, but Wiley stepped in front of him. "Calm down," he warned. "We still have the saucer, and we still have the admiral. We outwitted Picard only a few days ago; perhaps we can do it again. Even if Riker and La Forge managed to change the distress signal, the *Enterprise* still has no idea what's going on."

The commander needed several angry breaths to calm down. "All right. We've got to answer their hail and get them to dock. Maybe we can order them to do it. Somebody pick up Admiral Nechayev and put her in the command chair, but keep her tied up."

He snapped his fingers, and the big Bajoran rushed to obey his orders. Roughly, he scooped up the diminutive admiral, strode to the command chair, and dumped her into it. Nechayev struggled to sit up and regain some measure of her dignity. Fulton grabbed the disruptor pistol from Wiley and stepped behind the command chair.

Putting the muzzle of the weapon against the back of her skull, he hissed into her ear, "I'll blow your brains out if you don't do exactly as I tell you. Do you understand?"

Nechayev nodded, thin-lipped. "Contrary to what you think, I'm really not in a hurry to die."

"Good," said Fulton. "Simply order them to dock—that's all you have to do. Everyone else, move away from the command chair. When we go to visual, I want them to see just me and her. Will they be able to see my weapon?"

"No," answered the woman on Tactical. "I can adjust the field of vision."

"Do it." Fulton collected himself and plastered a pleasant smile upon his bland face. "Answer their hail and put us on screen."

Timothy Wiley's heart started pounding when he saw the stern visage of Captain Jean-Luc Picard appear on the main viewscreen. The captain of the *Enterprise* didn't look like the enemy, and he didn't look like a man who would be fooled or conquered easily.

"Captain," said Fulton pleasantly, "we've had some difficulties, as you have no doubt figured out. I don't know what went wrong with that simulation program. Anyway, if you dock with us, we can all get safely back to Starbase 211."

Picard frowned. "Are you sure you're all right? Where are Riker and La Forge?"

"Attending to some repairs." Fulton smiled. "As you can see, the admiral and I are fine."

"I've got a lot of questions," said Picard, "but I suppose we can get them answered later. Admiral, what is your take on this situation?"

All eyes turned to the sandy-haired admiral, who thus far hadn't budged so much as a centimeter. Wiley could see Fulton's clammy hand opening and closing around the grip of the disruptor as he pressed the barrel against her skull. Timothy Wiley held his breath.

"Captain Picard," said Admiral Nechayev with her usual bravado, "we've had some differences in the past, but I know that deep down you are a good officer who follows orders."

"Thank you, Admiral," Picard answered with uncertainty. Like everyone else, thought Wiley, he had no idea what was coming next.

She went on, "You are to listen very carefully to this order, and follow it to the letter."

"Yes, sir." Picard straightened to attention.

"You are to destroy this saucer section immediately, with all hands on board!"

Chapter Nine

TIMOTHY WILEY WHIRLED AROUND, expecting to see Admiral Nechayev's head disintegrate from a disruptor blast. But Henry Fulton could only gape at the admiral, dumbstruck by the order she had just given to destroy the saucer and everyone aboard it.

"Shields up!" shouted Wiley. "Fire phasers!"

The woman on Tactical pounded her console, and there was a high-pitched whine as she unleashed the saucer's phasers against the hull section. The viewscreen overhead crackled with static and went dark, replaced by a view of the hull section listing dramatically.

"Direct hit!" cried the officer.

Only then did Wiley turn his attention to Henry

Fulton. "Don't kill her!" he said. "She's still valuable."

Fulton glared at the man who was again giving the orders, and his grip tightened on the disruptor pistol pressed against Nechayev's head. Suddenly, he swung the weapon and bashed her across the back of the skull; she slumped to the deck, unconscious.

"Helm, evasive maneuvers!" ordered Wiley, striding across the bridge. "Tactical, order the *Shufola* to engage them, too!"

"Yes, sir!"

Picard staggered as the hull section was rocked by phaser fire, and he finally had to grip the back of Data's chair to stay on his feet. Having prepared to dock, their shields were down, and he cursed himself for his moment of hesitation following the admiral's unexpected order. But the captain couldn't believe that he had to destroy the saucer section with his comrades aboard.

"Shields up!" he barked.

Worf punched in the command but shook his head grimly. "Shields are up—but only forty percent. Shall I return fire?"

"Yes," said Picard, amazed that he was firing on a Federation vessel that contained several Starfleet officers.

Before Worf could even get a shot off, they were rocked again by enemy fire, and one of the consoles erupted in flame and smoke.

"Sir," said Data with his usual calm, "we are being fired upon by another ship—the freighter."

"Shields at six percent and failing," growled Worf. "Not enough power to use phasers!"

"Divert emergency power to shields," ordered Picard. "Helm, full reverse!"

"Aye, sir," said Tate. He could tell by the grimace on the young woman's face that the Conn was behaving sluggishly, but she hung with it and finally got the beleaguered vessel moving out of the dust cloud. Then they were pounded by another phaser blast, and Picard and Worf were both thrown to the deck.

Worf staggered to his feet, glanced at his console, and yelled, "Shields buckling!"

"Warp one, any course!" ordered Picard, scarcely believing that he was retreating from his own saucer section and a freighter.

Tate shook her head. "Warp engines do not respond."

With his jaw clenched, the captain made a difficult decision. He didn't want to obey the admiral's order and destroy the saucer, but he was prepared to do so. However, in their weakened state, they would be lucky to stage a retreat, let alone win this battle. What did these people want? Whoever had hijacked the saucer section, whoever was in that freighter—they hadn't gone to this much trouble to destroy the hull section. They *wanted* it, along with the saucer they already had.

"Worf," he said grimly, "hail them and offer to surrender."

"Sir?" asked the Klingon in amazement.

"Tell them we surrender."

"Yes, sir." With a look of extreme distaste on his

rugged features, Worf obeyed his captain's orders. After a moment, he reported, "Their terms are unconditional surrender."

The captain nodded. "Tell them we are lowering our shields in preparation to be boarded."

The Klingon looked as if he were swallowing his own bile. "Yes, sir."

"And, Mr. Worf," added the captain, "prepare a brace of six torpedoes. Target three for each craft."

"Yes, sir!" snapped the Klingon, much relieved. "Shields down, targeting torpedoes."

"Fire when ready." The captain turned to look at his viewscreen, and he could see a boxy green freighter emerging from the magenta cloud. The saucer section was apparently hanging back.

Worf grinned, showing his sharp, canine teeth. "Torpedoes away."

"Shields up!" shouted Picard. "Helm, evasive maneuvers!"

As the deck shifted under his feet, Picard glanced at his viewscreen just long enough to see three torpedoes plow in quick succession into the boxy freighter. The last one triggered an explosion that ripped the starscape, and the magenta cloud was soon joined by khaki-colored confetti that had once been a Pakled freighter.

"Vessel destroyed," Worf declared with satisfaction.

"Captain," said Data, "that was the same freighter we encountered on the Cardassian border."

The captain sighed heavily. "Well, they weren't so lucky this time."

He braced himself, expecting the saucer section to come roaring out of the cloud, blasting away with its phasers. If that happened, they had seconds left to live. He knew that saucer well. If they had gotten their shields up, there was no way that three torpedoes could make much of a dent. If the saucer attacked, the hull would be destroyed because it didn't have enough energy left to fight off a stiff breeze. At least they had fended off the attack for the moment, long enough to buy themselves a few seconds.

Without warp drive, there was nothing left to do but wait. Even if they survived the next few minutes, they had to pursue and destroy the saucer, killing Alynna Nechayev, Will Riker, and Geordi La Forge in the process. There were very few days in Picard's long and distinguished career when he wished he had stayed in France tending the vineyards with his brother Robert. However, this was one of those days.

"Damage report?" he asked testily.

Data's nimble fingers flew over his console, bringing up screen after screen of information. "There is a hull breech on decks thirty-one to thirty-three, sectors thirteen to seventeen, but containment fields are holding. The warp propulsion system has been disabled due to a leak in the primary deuterium tank, but impulse engines appear undamaged. We are encountering severe power fluctuations, and all emergency power has been diverted to the shields, which are holding at three percent. No casualties reported."

Picard remarked dryly, "No casualties. That's one advantage of having an empty ship. Can we get the warp engines back on line?"

"I believe so," answered Data. "It will take several hours, and we will have to divert power from other sources."

"Gather up Martinez and his crew, report to Engineering, and fix them. I'll take over on Ops."

"Yes, sir." Data snapped to his feet and strode toward the turbolift.

The captain sat down at the Ops station and studied the readouts, frowning. "That's odd. Sensors aren't showing any sign of the saucer inside the dust cloud."

"Could we have destroyed them?" asked Worf.

Picard shook his head. "It's hard to tell with the interference from that cloud. We'll have to go back in and take a look."

He glanced at Ensign Tate sitting beside him. "Helm, cease evasive maneuvers. Set course to last known position of the saucer section."

"Yes, sir."

"Proceed with caution, half impulse. Be ready to get out fast."

"Yes, sir."

Picard didn't really want to go anywhere with shields at only three percent, but he didn't have much choice. His orders were to destroy the saucer section with all hands on board, and no amount of anguish would change that order. But he had to find the saucer first. He glanced at the viewscreen and saw the dust cloud swirling like smoke around the twin nacelles. He wondered what astral body had come to an end so spectacular as to create this vast field of colorful debris.

Tate reported, "Sir, this is their last known location."

Picard looked at his sensors again, but they registered nothing, not even a trace of wreckage. He looked at the viewscreen and saw the same thing, then he gave a deep sigh as he reached the inevitable conclusion.

The rogue saucer had escaped.

On the bridge of the saucer, Timothy Wiley sat in stunned silence. The entire crew of the *Shufola*—Vylor, Mitchell, Enright, all the young, idealistic Maquis—were all dead. Blown to pieces before his eyes. It had never occurred to him, or the *Shufola,* that a Starfleet captain could be so treacherous. It made him realize that deep down there was no difference between Starfleet and the Maquis. When you were fighting for your life, there were no rules.

"So what now, Blue Moon?" asked Fulton, trying to sound cocky.

Wiley gazed up at the former Starfleet commander, hating him more with every passing moment. Although his own stupidity had let Riker and La Forge escape, Fulton had arrogantly called off the search for them. Without thinking it through, Fulton had put Nechayev on the viewscreen. In hindsight, there was only one thing such a woman was going to do, and she had done it. He glanced at her unconscious body on the deck, hoping that he would go to meet his death as bravely as she had.

He rubbed his eyes, thinking that maybe it wasn't Fulton's fault. Neither one of them were warriors, not like these people they were up against, not like the Architect, not like the Cardassians. Now their entire plan was shot, and Spencerville would remain in Cardassian hands. Not only that, but all they had was half a starship, the half without warp drive. The chances were looking grim that they would ever see their comrades and families in the demilitarized zone again.

"So what do we do now?" Fulton demanded.

Wiley leaped to his feet and grabbed the weasel, popping the pips right off his collar. "What do we do now? Now that our plan is shot to hell! So *now* you want to let *me* make the decisions? All right, Peacock, this is what we do."

He pushed Fulton away, and he stumbled and fell. *"You* take two of our crew and go find Riker and La Forge. You know this ship far better than any of us, so you find them. Got it?"

Fulton nodded meekly and staggered to his feet. "What are you going to do?"

"I'm going to reverse course and go back and *take* that hull. Just the fact that they haven't come after us means they're more banged up than we are. And without that hull section and warp drive, we're dead deep in Federation space."

Fulton cleared his throat. "Uh, there is another alternative. This saucer section can land safely on a planet, so if we can find an amenable planet, we could land there and hide out. I've got the codes to self-destruct the saucer—they would never find us."

Wiley laughed hollowly. "Why am I not surprised? So you want to forsake everything we stand for, just to hide out for the rest of your days? Never to fly the space lanes again, never to see the sun come up behind a planet. All right, we'll see what planets we could reach within our lifetime, and that will be plan B."

He pointed his finger at Fulton. "But your plan won't work either unless you find Riker and La Forge. So go find them, and don't come back here until you do."

A weary Will Riker slumped against a bulkhead and slid to the seat of his pants. He lifted his knees to try to get comfortable, but they felt as if they weighed a ton. Geordi stood watch at the window of the control booth of the main shuttlebay, an empty cavern without a single shuttlecraft in evidence. After hours of being on the run throughout the unfinished saucer section, Riker was still looking for a chair to sit in. He guessed he would never find one. They had picked the main shuttlebay as their latest hiding place because it would be impossible for anyone to sneak up on them. Plus, the self-contained booth allowed them to talk without fear of being overheard.

"What do you think happened up there?" asked Geordi, panting.

Riker shrugged. "Well, we know we were in a battle with another ship. We got knocked around pretty good back there. I guess the Maquis are not totally inept, because we're still in one piece."

"It felt like we got hit by photon torpedoes," said

the engineer. "If that was the captain, it must have gotten pretty desperate for him to fire on us."

"Yeah," said Riker somberly. "I wonder how they're doing? As far as weapons go, the hull section and the saucer section are an even match."

"At least we warned him off," said Geordi with relief. "But I hate not knowing what's going on."

The commander gave his comrade a grim smile. "Well, you could always go back to the bridge—they'll probably tell you."

Geordi shivered and stuck his hands under his armpits. "Is it my imagination, or is it getting cold in here?"

"Yeah, I noticed that, too," said Riker with concern. "What do you suppose is causing it."

The engineer frowned and rubbed his arms. "Well, if I had a huge ship like this and only a handful of crew to look for two escapees, I would try to flush them out."

Riker didn't like the sound of that. "And how would you do that?"

"I would shut off life-support on every deck, except the bridge, which is where I would keep my own people."

The commander rose wearily to his feet. "We're close to space in this shuttlebay. It would be one of the first places to get cold."

"We could survive the cold for a few hours, but we can't go long without oxygen."

Riker took a breath, wondering if his sudden weariness was due to a lack of oxygen, not physical exertion. There was no doubt in his mind that the temperature had dropped several degrees just in

151

the last few minutes. Geordi was right—there was no way a handful of Maquis could search the entire saucer section, but they didn't have to search it if they could force their prey into the open.

"How can we find out for sure?"

"I already know." Geordi pointed to a vent over their heads. "I can see air currents with my VISOR, and I don't see anything coming out of that vent. If this were a fully equipped saucer, there would be emergency oxygen supplies in the shelters, but those shelters are as empty as this shuttlebay."

"How long have we got?" asked Riker.

"Maybe twenty minutes before we pass out."

The commander paced the length of the tiny control booth. "All right, we haven't got any weapons, but we have our knowledge of the ship. This saucer has full life-support, doesn't it?"

"Yes," answered Geordi, "that's one place they couldn't fudge. There are life-support facilities on decks six, nine, and thirteen. You know, if we could get to the master console in any of those plants, we could restore life-support. That is, if they're not waiting for us there."

"What a choice," growled Riker. "We know they'll have people on the bridge, so we have to take a chance with life-support. You go to deck six, and I'll go to deck nine. If you have any suspicion that they're lying in wait for you, go to deck thirteen instead. We'll stay one step ahead of them."

Geordi chuckled. "This sounds like a trick I used to play on my poor old baby-sitter. Because I could see as well in the dark as the light, I used to run around and turn off all the lights in the house. As soon as she'd turn on the lights in one room, I'd turn them off in another room. Pretty lousy trick, huh."

"Yeah," said Riker fondly. He had known Geordi about as long as anyone in Starfleet, going all the way back to Starfleet Academy. If anyone was an all-around good guy, it was Geordi. That bit with the baby-sitter was probably the worst thing he had ever done to anyone. He didn't even cheat at poker when it was within his power.

"You get a head start," he said, watching his breath steam in the cold, thinning air. "If you get the life-support restored, meet back here."

"Yes, sir." Geordi swallowed. "See you later, I hope." He pressed the panel to open the door, then dashed down the stairs.

Riker sat on the top step and shivered for a minute, giving Geordi a head start. Then he padded down the stairs, opened the double doors, and peered into the corridor before stepping out. Just like every corridor he had seen on the prototype, this one was deserted and showed no sign of people ever traveling it. He steered away from the turbolifts in the central core to find a wide personnel lift that went directly from the shuttlebay to the mess hall two decks below. He strolled through the mess hall—just a white, sterile room on this craft—thinking that this saucer may have looked like the *Enterprise,* but it surely wasn't. Without the people, their noise, their dirt, and their energy, it wasn't really a ship at all. It was just a vast, hollow machine.

He took another short-haul lift that brought him

to the extensive life-support facilities on deck nine. He walked slowly down a narrow corridor, gazing through the observation windows on both sides of him, at rows upon rows of gleaming compressors, pumps, filters, heat exchangers, recycling units, storage tanks, all the equipment needed to generate and maintain a class-M atmosphere for a small city in space. On the walls of the enclosed rooms were banks of instruments and gauges. It was disconcertingly quiet down here, much more quiet than it should have been, and this time it wasn't just the absence of people. It was the absence of any kind of activity.

The commander passed the grids of a photosynthetic processing plant that reclaimed carbon dioxide from the air and added oxygen. It suddenly went dark behind the windows, and he flopped to his stomach. He breathed deeply, his lungs shooting blasts of steam into the air, and he told himself he had to remain calm. Behind him, every second room went dark, plunging the corridor into half-light. He waited for the sound of footsteps or disruptor fire, but the environmental deck was as quiet as before, only darker. It occurred to him that the Maquis had simply chosen that moment to dim some lights and save some energy. Or maybe it could even be Geordi, trying to send him a signal.

Riker waited, but his only company seemed to be the silent machines. Knowing that he didn't have enough time or enough air to panic, he dragged himself to his feet. He had to find the master controls, restart life-support, and get out. Luckily, the safety features on the environmental controls were all tilted in his favor, with an emphasis on getting life-support up and running, not shut down. But the Maquis would know where he was the moment he entered a command. As Geordi had prophesied, it would be a game of cat and mouse, running from one environmental deck to another.

The commander shook his head, trying to clear it and trying to remember where the master controls were. They would be close to the computer subsystems, he decided, and he knew where those were. Trying to control his breathing and his adrenaline, Riker started moving in a crouch. At an intersection in the narrow corridor, he hesitated then ducked to the left, stopping outside the first set of large double doors. They opened at his touch, and he walked inside, realizing that he wasn't dressed properly to enter. Even though positive air pressure kept the airflow moving outward into the corridor, a lightweight, class-8 cleanroom suit was required for working inside.

He laughed light-headedly. It was funny what odd thoughts occurred to you when you were desperate and trying to hold on to your consciousness. He looked around for the master console and found it nestled between two banks of process control computers. He laid his fingers upon the membrane keypad and tried to focus. It was very simple what he wanted to do—override whatever commands were in force and turn full life-support back on. Once they flooded the halls, staterooms, and corridors with fresh air, he and Geordi could hide out for several more hours. He began to enter his access code.

"Don't move," drawled a voice, "I've got a disruptor on you."

Riker peered over his shoulder to see the big Bajoran standing in the doorway, grinning at him. The Maquis soldier had scraggly hair on the crown of his head, crooked teeth, and a corroded earring dangling from the top of his right ear. He did indeed have a disruptor pistol trained upon Riker's midsection.

The Starfleet officer held his hands up, wondering if he should dive to the left or the right. "Can I turn around?" he asked.

"If you like to see yourself getting blasted, sure, turn around."

"You're awfully brave with that disruptor in your hand," said Riker. He kept his back to the armed man. "You'd probably prefer to shoot me in the back, so go ahead."

"Step away from the console," said the Bajoran.

"Oh, no, you can shoot it, too," answered the bearded officer. "As a matter of fact . . ."

He dove to his right, where there was a robotic tool cart, and the Bajoran fired his disruptor, ripping off the top half of the cart and blasting molten tools halfway across the computer room. Riker rolled to his back and kicked what was left of the flaming tool cart; it careened across the deck and slammed into the Bajoran's shins.

As he staggered back, yelping with pain, Riker scrambled behind shelves of tiny electrical parts. The Bajoran blasted a hole through the parts inventory, and bits of isolinear chips rained down like silicon hail. All Riker could do was flop to his stomach, trying not to heave too loudly for breath. Rubbing his shins, the Bajoran maneuvered himself between the two closest doors. He didn't have to be in any hurry, as there was no escape, except past him.

"Like I said," shouted Riker, "you're a big man with a disruptor! Good with your fists, too, if you've got somebody who's tied up!"

"You're not tied up now!" shouted the Bajoran, waving his pistol angrily. "But you're still cowering like some stinking Federation excuse for a . . ."

"I keep hearing the Maquis are brave! Throw that weapon away and face me like a man!"

"How about if I just put it in my belt?" asked the Bajoran. He slid the disruptor into a tailored holster on his belt and snapped a metal guard over it.

That was probably as much concession to fair play as Riker was going to get, so he bounded to his feet and looked around wondering if he could find something to use as a weapon.

"Come on, Mr. Commander, sir!" snarled the Bajoran, waving him on. "Just you and me."

Riker bulled toward him and took him down in a football tackle, head to the Bajoran's midsection. With satisfaction, he heard the air wheeze from the Bajoran's lungs as he batted away his flailing arms. He hated to hit a man when he was down, but he clocked the Bajoran on his thick jaw before he could recover his breath. Even in unconsciousness, the man gasped loudly in the rapidly thinning air. Riker panted, too, as he pushed the heavy body over and unbuckled the holster.

Riker staggered to his feet and buckled the deadly disruptor around his own hips, then shuffled back to the master controls. With what felt like the last of his energy, he finished restoring life-support to all decks. For good measure, he started to turn all the lights back on, too. Before he could finish that project, he heard the footsteps plodding toward him, and he whirled around to see the Bajoran charging like a wounded wildebeest, bleeting like one, too. The commander tried to spring out of the way, but he was too slow, and the mad Bajoran caught him in the stomach with a head butt and tossed him into a row of cabinets.

Now it was the human's turn to gasp for breath as he staggered to his feet, fumbling for the disruptor pistol on his waist. The Bajoran howled with rage at this affront and leaped upon Riker's back. The commander thrashed about in the computer room, trying to shake his tormentor, but he clung tight, trying to choke Riker and wear him down. When the Bajoran took a bite out of his shoulder, the human backed up hard against the bank of cabinets. The Bajoran lost his grip and fell to the floor, but amazingly started to rise again. Then Riker whirled around and caught the brute in the nose with a karate chop. Blood spurted as the man staggered back, and Riker licked his own mustache, tasting the dried blood from their earlier encounter.

Now Riker thought he would clear the pistol from his holster, but he was wrong. The Bajoran charged again, and they ended up wrestling like two bighorn sheep, locking antlers. Both of them staggered backward. The human slumped to the deck, barely clinging to consciousness, but he was revived by a cooling blast of air that suddenly shot from a floor vent. The environmental systems had kicked in! As the Bajoran tried to sit up, Riker crawled toward a computer workbench and hauled himself to his feet. He heard grunting and turned around to see the Bajoran also swaying on his feet.

They grimaced like animals as they slowly circled each other. There was no doubt in either man's bloodshot eyes that they would have to finish it this time.

As soon as Riker's hand moved toward his weapon, the Bajoran charged. Only the human never intended to draw—he feinted to his right and lashed out with his foot, catching the big man dead in the kneecap. He heard a sickening crunch followed by a guttural groan as the man collapsed to the deck. Finally Riker had ample time to draw his weapon.

As he backed away, his chest heaving, he knew that he could kill the Bajoran and probably should. He could tell from the man's dejected stoop and bowed head that he expected to die. But the commander knew too much about Bajor's recent history to take a Bajoran life so casually. At this point, the hatred of Cardassians was so ingrained in their psyche that they couldn't imagine life any other way.

Riker had to admit his own prejudice. To him, the Bajoran members of the Maquis were far more understandable than the human members, who were revolting against their own people. So he didn't pull the trigger on the disruptor. He holstered the weapon, limped out the door, and left the Bajoran to writhe in agony with a broken kneecap.

He shuffled down the corridor between alternating rooms of light and dark. Even if he hadn't turned all the lights back on, he had gotten the life-support systems working again, and he had shown himself and the Maquis that they weren't going to roll over and die. Somehow Riker didn't think the wounded Bajoran would try to tamper with the life-support systems himself. His bosses would have to send somebody else down here, which could take several minutes, and they would find the Bajoran. But they wouldn't find him.

Now that Riker had a weapon, he thought about waiting in ambush for them, but he decided not to. He had to pick his battles carefully, and he first wanted to know what the situation was topside. Fulton and the man called Blue Moon might still be fighting for supremacy, and maybe he could use their divisiveness against them. He had accomplished his immediate goal, and now it was time to make sure that Geordi was safe. As for the admiral, he tried not to think about her. She wasn't likely to last long at the hands of the Maquis.

The commander paused outside the turbolift, wondering if he should risk taking the common means of transportation. He opted instead for the Jeffries tube farther down the corridor, even if it meant taking a lot longer to travel from deck to deck.

Riker wasn't sure where he was going next, but

he did know one thing—he was done being a captive or a fugitive. From now on, it was time to go on the offensive.

Geordi La Forge crouched in total darkness, yet he could see the infrared streams of processed air pumping from the vents over his head. He made a fist and muttered, "All right, Commander, you did it."

He was stuck in a turbolift that had stopped suddenly, plunging him into total darkness. Lack of light was no problem for Geordi, but he had been driving himself crazy with worry over what had stopped the lift in the first place. He had spotted an armed Maquis guard on deck six, and he assumed that was where they had taken over control of life-support. He had gotten away without being spotted, or so he thought, but then the turbolift had quit on him, practically scaring him to death. Geordi had no idea whether he was trapped or just unlucky.

He supposed they could be turning off random systems in an effort to make something like this happen. On the other hand, maybe they had gone back into battle with Captain Picard, and this was shipwide damage. He didn't know, and the worst of it was he was getting used to not knowing.

Geordi swallowed, gulping as much of the fresh air as he could absorb, then he gazed up at the ceiling of the lift. He knew there were access hatches both above and below him, with the top one being impossible to reach without a ladder, and the bottom one requiring the removal of several delicate circuit boards and gel packs. Turbolifts were designed to be accessed from the outside—it never occurred to the designers that a person would be crazy enough to crawl *out* of a turbolift into the shaft. It was an extremely dangerous notion, because the lift could come back to life without warning, crushing a person in an instant.

So why was he thinking about it? Geordi rubbed his eyes and tried to figure out another plan, other than merely waiting and hoping that Riker could single-handedly keep life-support going. He kept coming back to the original foolishness—the idea of breaking out of the lift. If the principal danger were the lift coming back to life, then all he had to do was find a way to shut it down permanently. Then he could open a hatch and crawl out in relative safety.

He sat down in the darkness and tried to remember everything he knew about turbolifts. Somewhere in their numerous layers of redundant safeguards, there was a condition that would shut down the turbolift instantly, to such an extent that it would not be allowed to come back on until it was thoroughly checked. What were the conditions that would trigger such a radical reaction?

Hmmm, thought Geordi, *weightlessness.*

Each turbolift had its own artificial gravity generator, because the lifts moved between gravitational fields on the various decks. Even stopped at a deck, as this one was stubbornly stopped at the moment, the lift's own gravity subsystem took over. If he could get to the circuitry beneath his feet and disable the gravity generator, he would kill two birds with one stone! First he would cause a class-one shutdown—totally disabling the lift until the problem was corrected—plus he would be able to float to the roof and bounce out of this high-tech cage. It was worth a try.

Geordi crawled out of the way and pounded his fist on the right corner of a floor panel, which made the corner to his left jump slightly. He grabbed the protrusion. He thanked the currents of fresh air that flowed toward the negative pressure beneath the flooring, because they showed him where everything was in the dark.

He lifted the floorboard and leaned it carefully against the wall, trying not to make much of a sound. Then he inspected the circuitry and access panels. Everything in a Starfleet vessel was designed around the concept that artificial gravity had to be the last thing to go. Humanoids had never shown themselves the least bit adaptable to low gravity—they wasted away in it—so this precept was sacrosanct. In short, it was very serious business when the gravity went out.

Geordi took off his boot, lifted it high over his head, and punched the heel through an array of gel packs. He ignored the bioplasm that splashed upon his face, and he kept punching until he broke through the plastic membrane that protected the forcefield conduits. Those he smashed ruthlessly.

His legs lifted off the floor first, followed by his chest, and he had to grasp the frame of the flooring to stay long enough to finish his work. With skilled fingers, he ripped out a number of connectors that would trigger sensors all over the ship. Yes, the

Maquis would know where he was, but it was more important that the computer realize that things were really amiss on this turbolift.

He let go, pushed off, and floated in the dark to the ceiling of the turbolift. Although Geordi's peculiar kind of vision was good in the dark, it wasn't perfect, and he crashed headfirst into the ceiling. Little shards of glass floated all around him, tapping against his VISOR, and he quickly finished the job by smashing through what was left of the overhead panel. With a twist of a latch and a strong shove, he opened the hatch and felt the air and plastic shards rush past him into the vacuum of the turbolift shaft.

A scarier place on the *Enterprise* than an empty turbolift shaft would be hard to find. This one seemed to stretch for an eternity into empty blackness, and Geordi had no great desire to crawl out there. Yet he did, slithering through an opening that was designed for youthful ensigns.

As soon as he entered the shaft, he found himself being pulled toward the artificial gravity on the deck above him, which he figured was deck eleven. All he could do was protect his head with his arms as he floated toward the turbolift entrance on that deck. He bounced off a beam, catching most of the blow on his shoulder, then he grasped for any handhold to let him get to the door. He found the emergency override panel, and he couldn't think of any reason to stay inside the dismal turbolift shaft. In this stripped-down saucer there was probably nothing on deck eleven, although it would be gardens and greenhouses on the *Enterprise*. In this hollow imitation, he missed his real ship.

He punched the panel and opened the door, feeling himself get sucked toward the gravity. With great relief, Geordi sprang onto a solid deck with genuine artificial gravity!

Well, that was his last jaunt in a turbolift, thought Geordi, he would stick to the Jeffries tubes from now on.

Chapter Ten

IN THE DEMILITARIZED ZONE between Federation and Cardassian space, the ravaged planet of New Hope continued to burn. Three stories underground, a pale, slim Bajoran, who was called simply the Architect, in this lifetime, stopped decrypting a report from a Maquis cell near Spencerville. She looked up wearily from her desk, tense and nervous but not knowing why until her underground post was rocked by a solid strike on the planet's surface. The lights crackled on and off, and chunks of the ceiling fell all around—big clods of mud and molten minerals.

The Cardassians were back with their thermal weapons!

She dashed out the doorway and collided with

one of her human confederates; the blond woman stumbled, gripped her arm, and stared vacantly at her. As the walls melted around them, the Bajoran took the woman by the shoulders and shook her until her panic was replaced by anger.

"Let go of me!" demanded the woman. "Can't you see, we're under attack!"

"A random attack," said the Architect. "They don't know our exact location." It was hard to sound convinced of that, with the ground quaking all around them and superheated mud pelting them from the ceiling. The Bajoran tried to deny it, but she couldn't—their post had been compromised, and they had to desert it or risk being buried alive!

"Okay, we'll evacuate!" the Architect shouted. "Round up everyone and get them to the sleds."

"The sleds." The blond woman nodded as if she understood.

"Yes! I'll destroy our files. Get going!" The Architect shoved the woman down the corridor, then dashed in the opposite direction. There wouldn't be enough time to destroy all the backup files—the maps, intelligence reports, and research that had accumulated over the months—but she could shovel the bulk of it into the furnace. The files were encrypted, but a lot of them related to Spencerville; and the last thing she wanted was to tip their hand over that operation.

With a sizzling thud, a glop of molten ceiling dropped upon her cheek, and she shrieked and leaped back as the whole ceiling gave way over her head. Gasping for breath and battling away the debris with her burned hands, the Architect scuttled away from the collapsing corridor. That was when she knew for certain that they would have to leave everything behind—they couldn't destroy any of it! The records would probably be buried in the mud, but she despised the idea of leaving anything behind for Cardassians to find.

"Architect!" shouted one of her comrades from the stairwell. "Come on!"

She was torn between obeying her common sense or her duty, when more of the ceiling began to give way. Fleeing for her life, she hurled herself into the gleaming titanium stairwell and stumbled after her comrades. If only she could collapse the entire underground complex—with a bomb or something. The Architect was still trying to figure out how to destroy the complex when two Cardassian goons materialized in the stairwell only a floor beneath her. She was able to duck out of sight, but the man who had come back for her, Jason, was caught in the wrong place. As he tried to draw his weapon, the Cardassians promptly murdered him on the stairs.

From her vantage point above them, she was invisible as she hefted her new disruptor pistol for the first time. As Blue Moon had told her, these weapons had no stun settings. Peering down at the Cardassians, their bony skulls appeared like bull's-eyes in the centers of their bodies, and the Bajoran fired without a moment's hesitation. She cut one of them down with a quick burst, but the other one dove out of sight. As she pounded down the stairs after him, she caught the glimmering reflection of a transporter beam. He had escaped, leaving his dead companion, but now the death squads knew there was a Maquis cell down here.

Quickly she rifled the body of the dead Cardassian, trying to ignore the scorched crown of his head, where she had plugged the bull's-eye. She pocketed his hand weapon, threw back his vest, and found a treasure trove strapped to his chest—a weapons belt complete with four grenades.

She picked a grenade at random and climbed painfully back to the level she had just left, where the air was stifling and even the titanium looked faded from the onslaught of heat. The Architect could barely open the door, and a blast of hot air sent her staggering back. Nevertheless, she squeezed the trigger on the grenade, grabbed the handrail for support, and flung the bomb as far into the inferno as she could. Then she ran like hell, leaping three or four steps at a time until she tripped and sprawled at the bottom of the stairwell.

She cringed, waiting to be buried by the resulting explosion, but nothing happened. Then she saw a slight breeze bang the door shut overhead. The only trouble was, she had never seen a breeze in these tunnels before.

Gas! The Bajoran staggered to her feet, feeling a jab of pain in her right ankle. With gas sealing off the top level, she really had to admit that the records were at risk. There was nothing overt in the pile of isolinear chips, but if they cracked the encryption, the Cardassians might think there were an awful lot of tourist photos of Spencerville.

Cursing her lack of planning, the Architect

limped from the stairwell into the cool, dark air of the sled chute. During the heyday of New Hope, trash was disposed of deep underground and ferried there by gondolas on rails, known for decades as sleds. If you didn't mind the lingering stench and the petrified garbage sticking to the inside panels, the sleds offered a cheap, efficient, and ready-made transportation system, long forgotten by the Cardassians.

Or so the Architect hoped.

She joined three of her shell-shocked friends in the last sled, noting with relief that the first two sleds had already departed. She climbed in, thinking the conveyance was shaped more like a rowboat than a sled, although she scarcely knew much about either one.

The blond woman gazed wearily at her. "Where's Jason?"

The Architect shook her head and looked down as she tied a rope around her waist, which was the best she could do for a seat belt. "He's not coming."

"No!" cried the blond woman, jumping to her feet. Her friends quickly yanked her back down, and they were so distracted with her plight that they didn't see the four Cardassians materialize outside on the loading dock. Luckily, their voices carried in the cool darkness, and their eyes needed a moment to adjust to dreary surroundings.

"Down!" breathed the Bajoran, pushing the woman in front of her to the floor. "Let's go! Get moving!"

At the front of the sled, a brawny Maquis jumped up, grabbed the brake lever, and yanked it back. The car shifted abruptly and rumbled along the rail, drawn toward the first magnetic link in the chain. Two of the Cardassians whirled around and discharged their weapons at the sound, and their beams ricocheted off the walls of the chute. The Architect returned fire with her disruptor, shooting indiscriminately and missing, but she sent the invaders scurrying for cover.

With the sled drawing away at a maddeningly slow pace, the Bajoran kept shooting, just trying to keep the attackers from taking careful aim. One of them leaped to his feet and shot wildly; their beams crisscrossed over the sled rails, exploding with a shimmering arc that illuminated the dreary, underground junkyard.

As the Cardassians ducked for cover, the Bajoran remembered her gas grenades. With the sled picking up speed, she yanked a grenade from her belt, squeezed it, and hurled it as far as she could. It bounced on the loading dock and detonated with a slight fizzle; the Cardassians collapsed before they even knew what had hit them. The gas probably wasn't fatal, thought the Architect, because Cardassians loved to take prisoners, whom they could torture at their leisure.

They picked up speed in the rickety conveyance and plunged into abject darkness. The Bajoran felt her teeth rattle as they bounced over bad welds in the old rails, careened around corners, and raced down the chute, *whoosh*ing from one magnetic field to another. There was no way of knowing if they were going up or down except for the queasy sensation in her stomach.

She had delighted in this wild ride before, but today she could only feel remorse and a terrible sense of loss. The loss of Jason bothered her, even though death had become a constant in their lives; but on an even deeper level she mourned the death of her naïveté, her foolish belief that they had been safe in the bowels of New Hope. The Cardassians even scoured their own waste looking for the Maquis. How could they fight such a craven enemy? Maybe the Federation had been cowardly but practical when they deserted the colonists to make peace with the ravenous dogs.

The Bajoran peered into the darkness and thought she saw a yellow light glimmering in the distance. Even though escape was looking plausible, she felt no relief. Everything they had worked for was now jeopardized, and it was back to the beginning for her if she got out of here alive. She supposed there would always be a use for a Galaxy-class starship if that part of the operation proved successful.

Her part was a failure. In all likelihood, there would not be a hundred thousand Cardassians killed in one fell swoop. A city would not be leveled, families would not perish, and the Cardassians would not be put on notice that they couldn't keep what they had stolen. The Architect panted for breath in the dank chute, feeling the sled jerk up an incline and start to brake. She wouldn't slaughter a hundred thousand Cardassians, and she didn't know whether to laugh or cry about it.

She felt tired, drained way beyond her short span of years. This was a time when she should be teaching the future generations, maybe teaching her own children, but she was running for her life . . . again. Sometimes it felt as if she was trapped in a nightmare, a place of never-ending war and strife. Yet it was her choice to be here, and the times when she'd had happiness, she had tossed it away. She blinked back tears and screwed her eyes shut.

The smell alone let her know they were coming to pit six, their exit from this line. She tried not to look at the yawning hole on her left, still smelling ripe decades after reaching capacity, the universe's biggest compost heap. She braced herself for a sudden stop as her sled piled into the one in front of it, and she wasn't disappointed. Strong arms were soon pulling her out of the sled, for which the Architect was grateful, because her sprained ankle was already swelling. She grabbed someone's shoulder and limped toward the shuttlecraft that was waiting in pit seven, where the garbage had been hardened by microbes introduced by the Maquis. Now it was as hard and smooth as salt flats.

She grimaced in pain as she climbed a ladder and stepped inside the shuttlecraft's crowded cabin. They made room for their wounded commander and shoved her into a window seat in the second row. Ten exhausted people scrambled aboard and slumped wherever they happened to land, and the door wasn't even shut when the pilot fired his thrusters.

They bucked up the big chute, the one the Maquis had blasted out between two sled chutes. Normally the Bajoran would be deep in conversation and not paying the slightest attention to this flight, but her eyes were fixed on the tiny porthole, watching the rocks whiz by. She was fearful that the Cardassians had destroyed this tunnel, too, with their thermal blasters, and the shuttlecraft would be swallowed in mud. She wanted to make sure the pilot was checking his sensors, but she didn't have enough energy to lift her head off the window. The Architect had burns on her face and hands, and her hair was both muddy and singed, so she was glad that nobody wanted to talk to her.

Cardassian vessels had to be orbiting the planet. She couldn't think about them—the pilot only had to get to warp drive, and they would escape from the DMZ into Federation space. That presented its own problems, but they were minor compared to being chased through the DMZ by Cardassian death squads.

They broke through the camouflage netting that covered a bomb crater a hundred kilometers outside the city limits. The sky was still brown out here, marveled the Architect, but it wasn't shot through with flames and smoke. As they rose higher, the sky actually turned blue, and escape from the nightmare seemed possible.

The shuttlecraft made a hard bank, an evasive maneuver, and the passengers were tossed out of their seats. The Bajoran yelped with pain as she came down on her ankle, but she bit her lip and crawled back into her seat. Whatever the pilot had swerved to avoid, he must have missed it, because they were still in one piece. The craft picked up speed and blasted through the stratosphere, and all the Architect saw out her window were blinding streaks of sun. She closed her eyes, because if a photon torpedo got them in the last leg of their escape, she didn't want to see it coming.

She was almost surprised when she felt the shudder of entering warp drive. Warp one was the best the old personnel shuttlecraft could do, but it should be good enough, she told herself, to make the short hop to Federation space.

After that, the problem would be getting back into the DMZ through the Federation blockade.

Captain Picard started to pace again and quickly stopped himself. It was a good thing that the deck of the battle bridge was manufactured from impervious tripolymers, or else he would have worn a trench in it from all his pacing. He wanted his own bridge and his own ship back, but he would settle for having warp drive again.

Data had commandeered all of the skeleton crew for the repair effort, leaving only Picard, Worf, and Ensign Tate on the bridge. As power was still fluctuating, the hull section hadn't moved from the Thresher Dust Cloud since repairs began several hours ago. With shields at three percent, no warp drive, and not enough power for phasers or communications, the captain couldn't be blamed for not risking his vessel further. But there was a ship out there that he had been ordered to destroy, and it was getting away, while they sat around and licked their wounds.

He pounded his fist into his palm and looked up to find Worf watching him. The Klingon quickly looked down at his instruments, and Picard began to pace again, despite his resolve not to. They had been given a direct order by Admiral Nechayev to destroy the saucer, yet they had let it escape. With warp drive, they could have hounded it. Even if the hull could not have attacked, at least it could have kept Starfleet informed of the saucer's whereabouts. They hadn't even done that much.

Picard couldn't help but wonder, had the enemy been Romulans or Borg, would he have pursued them, fighting down to the last shield and the last torpedo? Or would he have hesitated as he did, which was why his ship suffered so much initial damage in the exchange of fire. In the saucer were his friends, comrades, and a superior—he could destroy it, but not without hesitation. His hesitation was only human.

Picard sighed. He was also waiting for the genuine saucer section to rendezvous with them, but the saucer could be many more hours en route to this destination. Having the saucer would give him a weaponry advantage, but it would tax his energy reserves and give him no more speed than impulse power. Still, he couldn't sit here any longer, doing nothing.

The captain jutted his chin and tapped his comm badge, "Picard to Data. Report."

"Yes, Captain. Repairs on the warp drive are seventy-three percent complete, and we are nearing completion on several other critical subsystems. We have been hampered by a lack of skilled technicians and the absence of certain replicator codes. We have had to use some components which are specified for other units."

"Why didn't we have all the codes?"

"They are part of the saucer section's inventory."

"Of course, the saucer section," muttered Picard. "Data, we have full impulse power, don't we?"

"Yes, sir. However, using impulse engines is not advisable with our current power fluctuations. It may produce unpredictable consequences with shields, sensors, communications, and weaponry."

"We have to chance it," said Picard, "I want to catch up with that saucer section."

"Sir," cautioned Data, "without warp drive, the chances of catching the saucer are minimal."

"They don't have warp drive either, and we got in a few licks. Perhaps they had to stop, too. Stay with the repairs, Data, but keep the impulse engines on-line—I may call for them. Picard out."

The captain strode behind Tate and looked over her slim shoulder. "Ensign, is there any sign of the saucer section?"

"No, sir. Long-range sensors remain inoperative."

Where would they go? Picard wondered. *Back to*

the DMZ? No, that's too far without warp drive. This deep in Federation space, they might want to hide. "What is the closest class-M planet?" he asked Tate.

Tate accessed the ship's computer. "That would be Pedrum, inhabited by a society that is equivalent to Earth's early Iron Age. Contact is disallowed, and Prime Directive restrictions apply."

"Take us out of the cloud at half impulse," ordered Picard, "then set course for Pedrum at full impulse. It's just a guess, but at least we'll be doing something to find them."

"Yes, sir."

"Mr. Worf, can you raise Starfleet yet."

"No, sir," muttered the Klingon. "Subspace is still inoperative."

"Keep trying." Picard turned his attention to the viewscreen and watched the magenta waves of dust part before the sweeping hull of the *Enterprise.* He could imagine the view from outside the ship as the graceful nacelles sliced through the giant fingers of phosphorescent dust. There was beauty here, but too much danger, and he hoped he would never see the Thresher Dust Cloud again.

The turbolift doors slid open and Guinan stepped onto the bridge carrying a tray of steaming mugs.

"Are you allowed to drink coffee on the bridge?" she asked.

"No," snapped Beverly and Deanna in unison,

both sounding rather testy about it. In retrospect, they had brought too few crew members for a trip of this length without warp drive.

Guinan shrugged. "Just thought I'd ask."

Beverly Crusher swiveled around in the command chair. "Gherink, I need the location of the class-M planet that is closest to the Thresher Dust Cloud."

The doctor tapped a finger to her lip. "And, Deanna, run a short-range scan of the dust cloud and the surrounding area. We're getting close enough now that we might be able to spot something."

"Aye, sir," said the counselor, sitting a bit straighter at the Conn.

"I'll try hailing them again," said Beverly, rising from the command chair and marching down to the Ops console.

Finally the computer responded to Gherink's request, and she squinted at her readouts. "The closest class-M planet is called Pedrum. It's inhabited, and there are a lot of warnings about the Prime Directive."

"Then it must be an emerging technology," answered Beverly. "Let's hope everybody stays far away from it." She shook her head. "They still don't respond to hails. Where are they?"

"Wait a second," said Deanna Troi, blinking at her readouts. "Sensors show something—it might be a ship—behind the Thresher Dust Cloud and approaching at full impulse."

"What kind of ship?"

"I can't tell for sure," admitted Deanna, "the interference from the dust cloud is affecting our sensors. It might be just a reflection, but it looks like a ship."

Beverly punched up a new setting for the viewscreen, and they got their first good look at the Thresher Dust Cloud, which looked colorfully foreboding, like a ball of cotton candy floating in space. Guinan wouldn't mind having an outfit that color, but she didn't want to be lost inside it with nothing else to look at.

"What's the status of the other ship?"

"They just broke through the cloud," answered Deanna. "They are headed in our direction, intercept course."

"Still no identification?"

"No, sir."

"Tactical, it won't do any good, but try hailing them."

"Yes, sir," answered Mason. "Hailing frequencies are open." After a moment, he shook his head. "No response."

Gherink took her eyes away from her science station to watch both the main viewscreen and the acting captain. They were approaching a ship that was probably their own, maybe even the other half of the *Enterprise,* still it was a tense few minutes as the ships drew closer at full impulse. Gherink occasionally ran her sensors, but the dust cloud was still distorting the signal.

The doctor sat stiffly in the command chair and shook her head. "These may be our own people, but something's wrong here. Tactical, put our shields up."

"Yes, sir, shields up."

Guinan thought she saw Beverly breathe a little easier after issuing that order. "Ops, put the ship on screen."

"Yes, sir," answered the ensign at Ops. "On screen."

Once the officer had narrowed the field of vision to include nothing but the approaching ship, everyone on the bridge bolted upright in their seats. They stared at a mirror image of themselves—a saucer section minus its hull. Even though they expected to find such a vessel out here, actually coming in contact with one was an eerie experience.

"Can we ID that vessel?" asked Beverly.

"Yes, sir," replied the ensign. "They're far enough beyond the dust cloud that we now have positive ID. That is the prototype saucer."

"Then why aren't they answering our hails?" Beverly rose from the command chair, strode toward the viewscreen, and crossed her arms, staring at it. "Where's the hull section?"

"There are life-sign readings on the saucer section!" Gherink exclaimed. "Ten of them."

"They're alive," said Beverly. "Well, that's good news. What is our time until intercept?"

"Five minutes," answered Ops.

"We're closing rapidly," said Deanna. "Permission to reduce speed."

Beverly nodded. "Go to one-third impulse. Keep hailing them."

"One-third impulse," said Deanna.

With a relieved sigh, the ensign at Ops reported, "They've slowed to one-third impulse."

"Full stop," ordered Beverly. "Let's not get too close. We can't dock with them, after all."

The enormous saucer, blinking importantly from stem to stern, filled their entire viewscreen.

"We're stopped at a thousand kilometers distance," said Deanna. "Within transporter range."

"Open all channels and put me on screen," ordered Beverly. "Prototype saucer, this is the *Enterprise.* Please respond to our hails. We are concerned about your status. Repeat, please respond to our hails."

As if in answer, a grainy image appeared on their viewscreen, showing what looked like Admiral Nechayev lying unconscious and bloody in front of the command chair. The frame widened to show another Starfleet officer, staggering to his feet behind the command chair. Nobody else was visible on their bridge.

"I'm Commander Henry Fulton!" he said, panting for breath. "We need immediate assistance. Can we . . . can we beam over to your sickbay?"

"Yes," said Beverly without hesitation. "Prepare to lower shields."

Chapter Eleven

"WAIT A MINUTE!" shouted Gherink, looking closely at her life-sign scans. "Put them on hold for a moment."

Beverly nodded to Mason, and he temporarily cut off the transmission.

"According to these life-sign readings," said the Deltan, "two of those people over there are Bajorans. Did any Bajorans ship out with the hull and prototype?"

Beverly racked her brain trying to remember whom she had seen at the briefing, the one from which she and Deanna had been excluded. "They were all regular crew, I thought, except for the admiral and Fulton."

Gherink nodded. "But, sir, as I recall we only

had one Bajoran on the *Enterprise,* and she's gone."

"Do *not* lower shields," ordered Beverly Crusher. "Go ahead, put them back on screen."

Her screen lit up with the grainy image of the bridge and two senior Starfleet officers slumped on the deck, both now appearing to be unconscious.

"I need to speak to Commander Riker immediately," said Beverly, trying not to be influenced by their apparently desperate plight. "Or Commander La Forge."

Fulton rose weakly on one elbow. "I'm the only one who's conscious," he moaned. "Just lower your shields. . . . Beam over the admiral at least."

"He's lying," said Deanna under her breath.

"But that is Admiral Nechayev, isn't it?" asked Beverly.

The Betazoid nodded.

"Tactical," said the doctor, "relay our situation back to Starfleet and request they advise."

While she was giving that order, Commander Fulton struggled to his knees. He paused and seemed to wave to someone beyond the field of vision. Suddenly the viewscreen turned a blinding white, and the main bridge of the *Enterprise* was rocked, knocking Beverly off her feet.

"Phaser attack!" shouted Mason at the Tactical station. "Shields holding!"

"Helm, full reverse," said Beverly, gripping her chair. "Mason, can we fire back without risking our shields?"

"Yes, sir."

"Full phasers, fire when ready!"

* * *

In a Jeffries tube on the prototype saucer, Will Riker was just stepping down to a lower rung when a sudden jolt jarred him loose and sent him swinging over the mouth of the vertical tunnel. He shouted as he lost his grip with one hand and held on by a mere three fingers of the other one. On his return swing, he extended his free hand far enough to grab an upper rung, letting go with his bottom hand and crashing into the ladder. He almost lost consciousness before he could lift his feet onto the rungs and catch his breath.

"Commander!" he heard a voice shout somewhere far below him. "Are you all right?"

"That you, Geordi?" he breathed. He didn't have much lung power left, and he didn't want to shout in this echo chamber.

"It's okay, I think we're alone in here." Geordi emerged from a connecting horizontal tube and started to climb toward Riker. "The way you shouted, good thing I wasn't Maquis."

"That jolt took me by surprise. What do you think happened?"

"I'd say we were fired upon," answered Geordi, climbing steadily toward him. "Our new captain is not very good at staying out of trouble. Hey, nice job getting the life-support back on. I got stuck in a turbolift."

"I'm tired of hiding and running," muttered Riker. "I want to go on the offensive. Strike back at them."

Geordi stopped a meter below him and nodded

in agreement. "I'm tired of not knowing what's going on. We could have a hull breach a hundred meters wide, and we wouldn't know it until we got off on the wrong deck—and got sucked into space."

"I wonder how the admiral is doing?" Riker grimaced as he touched his tender jaw.

Geordi lowered his head. "Yeah, I felt bad that I couldn't get both of you when I had the chance. My fault."

"No one's fault," said Riker. "When it comes to admirals, we don't have much luck. Still, we should try to rescue her, especially while they're engaged in battle."

"How?"

"Why not the same way as before?"

The chief engineer gripped the ladder in the crook of his arm and thought about the question. "We know they can't guard all of the transporter rooms, so we could probably get another chance to beam her out. But to beam intraship, you have to have exact coordinates—slip up and we put somebody inside a bulkhead. Since we ditched our comm badges, what can we use to fix the coordinates?"

Riker gulped, wishing he had some water. "I just know that we have to do something, and this is a good place to start. What could we use as a transporter beacon?"

Geordi's brow furrowed up to his VISOR. "Something small with its own transmitter. Listen, we haven't hit sickbay yet—let's go there."

"Lead on," answered the commander, discovering a cut on his ear. "I could use a first aid kit."

Nine decks over their heads on the bridge of the prototype saucer section, Timothy Wiley gently pounded his fist on the armrest of the command chair. Once again, he had let Henry Fulton's arrogance jeopardize the operation, in fact, all of their lives! He had wanted to avoid the other saucer section and stay in pursuit of the hull section, as planned. But Fulton had insisted that they confront the other saucer, to keep them from alerting Starfleet, he said. He had been so certain that he could talk them into lowering their shields and then cripple them with one blast. The saucer would then be another prize for the Maquis to claim later, he assured them, and it would only take a moment.

Instead, the *Enterprise*'s saucer section was chasing them through the Thresher Dust Cloud at full impulse.

Wiley tried to think of a way to defeat it, or at least slow it down long enough to resume his chase of the hull section. But the saucer's captain knew the capabilities of these vessels better than he did; her ship was a mirror image of his own, down to the armrest he was beating with his fist. Without the element of surprise, he had no plan, no edge. Even if he defeated this woman's ship, it wouldn't do him any good—the saucers were two identical halves that did not make a whole.

Wiley blamed Henry Fulton for drawing the other saucer into the fray, but maybe it couldn't be avoided. He looked down to see the commander hovering over Admiral Nechayev, trying to revive her, but she remained steadfastly unconscious. Fulton finally gave up trying to revive her and went back to applying an antiseptic lotion to the cuts and bruises on her face, as if his concern would absolve him from his treachery.

Fulton looked like a beaten man himself, a person who had run out of both courage and sanity at the same time. But the freighter pilot had a hard time feeling pity for a man who had wasted precious time and gotten a second Federation starship on their tail!

"Get up, Fulton," he said with disgust. "Leave her. Go back to looking for Riker and La Forge."

Fulton gazed absently at the man in the command chair. "They won't really kill Admiral Nechayev," he whispered. "They'll let us go."

"No, they won't!" scoffed Wiley. "They'll hunt us down and kill us, just like she ordered them to. These are people who obey orders before they obey their own minds. Maybe they'll capture us, if they can, but I don't think they'll try very hard."

"Did you find it?" asked Fulton, gazing at the damnable magenta cloud in the viewscreen.

"Find what?" scowled Wiley.

"The closest class-M planet."

The young man looked back at his crewmate on the Science console. "Linda, you said you found a planet. What's the status of that?"

The woman hunched over her controls for a moment, reviewing past screens of data. Wearily she answered, "The planet is called Pedrum. It's class-M with plenty of water and vegetation. In fact, it's inhabited. We can't go there."

"Why not?" demanded the big Bajoran.

The woman looked askance at her comrade. "Prime Directive reasons. If we land there, we could influence a primitive society—they're only in the Iron Age. We might give them technology and knowledge way before they're ready for it."

"Is there another suitable planet within a reasonable distance?" asked Wiley.

The Maquis officer shook her head. "No, nothing close. Or nothing close to being class-M."

The Bajoran pounded his fist on his console. "Who cares about their stupid directives—just save our lives!"

"Yes," roared Fulton. "That planet is our destiny! Set course for Pedrum."

The woman shook her head and appealed to Wiley for support. "We can't land there. It's *inhabited!*"

Timothy Wiley brushed back his mustache and looked as if he had eaten something distasteful. "Listen, people, our options are limited. We've got two Federation ships to deal with, and there could be more on the way. Our main weapon, the element of surprise, is gone, and so is our rescue ship, the *Shufola.* We don't have warp drive and we aren't likely to get it. So here are our choices—give ourselves up and go to prison, die fighting the *Enterprise,* or land on Pedrum and hope we can escape into this primitive culture."

He looked pointedly at Linda Johnson, the young woman at the Science station. "Maybe we can land the saucer in a sparsely inhabited region. Fulton says that he has the codes to self-destruct, so maybe they won't find it." Wiley paused and looked thoughtful. "It's funny, but the Prime Directive actually works in our favor, because Starfleet can't mount a full-scale search for us. I've always respected the Prime Directive, but this is a matter of survival."

The young woman looked away in disgust, and Wiley turned toward the Tactical station, where the big Bajoran was bouncing on one leg, with his other leg in a makeshift splint. "Send a coded, subspace message to our cell," ordered Wiley. "Tell them that we aborted the mission and had to land on Pedrum. Maybe they'll be able to send a rescue party for us someday."

"Aye, sir," muttered the Bajoran, grimacing in pain as he dragged himself closer to his console.

"We're emerging from the dust cloud," said the officer on the Conn.

"Set course for Pedrum." Wiley thought about their new destination, the place where they would be spending the rest of their lives, if they were lucky. He had heard the term Iron Age any number of times, but he really couldn't imagine how primitive that was. Unfortunately, he wasn't a scientist with a wealth of knowledge he could parlay into a new career as an alchemist or magician. What he knew were interstellar freighters, which were probably in short supply in the Iron Age. Then again, they had sent a message to the Maquis, and perhaps there would be a rescue party someday. More than likely, thought the young man, they would end up as a bunch of mysterious corpses in a crashed UFO.

Without warning, the turbolift doors opened, and Commander William Riker stepped out, holding his hands over his head in the classic pose of surrender. "Don't shoot!" he begged, groveling. "I'm unarmed."

The big Bajoran started toward him, but his swollen kneecap made him think better of it. "He's not unarmed," warned the Bajoran, "he's got my disruptor!"

"No!" said Riker thrusting his hands higher. "I threw it away—go ahead and search me. I exhausted it trying to blast through a turbolift. I failed, and Geordi died anyway."

Wiley drew his own disruptor and moved warily toward the Starfleet officer. "Commander La Forge is dead?"

"Yes, he was crushed in a turbolift that malfunctioned."

Fulton cackled with laughter. "That was *my* doing!" As everyone stared at the madman, he shrugged and turned his attention back to the fallen admiral.

Riker took a step toward them. "The admiral, how is she?"

"That's not your concern," said Wiley. "Stay back."

"Really, Captain, I don't have any weapons. I just want to see how she is." With a look of concern on his bearded face, Riker moved closer to the unconscious woman.

"Hold it right there!" Wiley's stern tone of voice

finally froze the commander in his tracks, and the acting captain motioned to his Maquis compatriots. "Search him and tie him up."

They did a thorough job of searching the commander. They threw him into a spare chair on the bridge and were starting to tie him up when the officer on Ops shouted, "Our sensors have picked up the hull section! Dead ahead—between us and Pedrum."

"Put it on screen," ordered Wiley with a delighted grin. "Maybe we're going to get a second chance at them after all."

While everyone was distracted, Riker broke out of the grasp of the Maquis and rushed to Admiral Nechayev's side. Wiley leveled his disruptor and was about to fire when he saw that all the commander was doing was brushing Nechayev's hair back behind her ear. Fulton smiled beatifically at him, as if they were old friends who had come to pay their respects. Two Maquis rushed to grab Riker, and they hauled him rudely back to his seat.

Wiley glared at the first officer. "I have risked our mission out of compassion for you and the admiral, but we can't afford that anymore. I'll shoot you myself if you move again."

"Sorry," said Riker. "None of this was my idea. You know, we might all be alive tomorrow if you just surrendered."

The young man scowled at the truth of Riker's statement then looked back at the viewscreen, where the three-pronged image of the hull section was beginning to take shape. They were still traveling toward Pedrum and apparently hadn't spotted either of the approaching saucers. Maybe, thought Wiley, their sensors were damaged. After all, they had pounded the hull at point-blank range with her shields down, and it must have had some effect.

"Slow to half impulse," ordered Wiley, "let the other saucer catch up."

The Conn officer gave him a peculiar look but completed the command. "Half impulse," he reported.

"Now," Wiley said, a grin slowly spreading over his face, "input code Delta-6000."

The conn officer looked even more puzzled.

"We can overide their sensors, at least temporarily," Wiley explained patiently. "With any luck, we can produce a false image so that they can't distinguish our saucer from theirs."

Wiley was so pleased with his own cleverness that he almost didn't hear the strange keening sound in the still air of the bridge. By the time he looked down at Admiral Nechayev, she was vanishing in a glittering transporter beam. He drew his disruptor and was about to fire when he realized he was too late to stop her passive escape. He whirled toward Riker and couldn't fire at him either, because one of his own people stood directly behind the commander, who was quickly becoming as insubstantial as a ghost.

The last thing to disappear was the triumphant smile on Commander Riker's face.

As soon as he materialized on the transporter pad, Riker bent down and picked up the limp body of Admiral Nechayev. He strode off the transporter platform, past Geordi at the controls, then rushed out the door. He glanced back only long enough to make sure that the engineer had grabbed the first aid kit they had taken from sickbay, along with the disruptor pistol. The way things were going, they would probably need both.

There was no time for conversation, as they knew the Maquis could easily trace the transporter signal. So they had to put as much distance between themselves and the transporter room as possible. Unfortunately, Admiral Nechayev was in no condition to climb a Jeffries tube and Geordi wouldn't take another turbolift, so they had decided to head back to one of their original hiding places, the empty main shuttlebay. With any luck, the Maquis were too preoccupied at the moment to send more than a token force after them.

Riker hefted the admiral's body, getting a firmer grip on her slim torso, and made a sharp turn in the corridor. Geordi drew his disruptor to cover Riker. Without incident, they charged through the double doors of the main shuttlebay. While Geordi secured the doors, Riker carried his burden straight up the stairs and into the control booth. He gently set the unconscious admiral on the floor and gulped for breath.

Geordi came through the door a moment later, set the first aid kit on the floor, and opened it. "How is the ship?" he asked, unable to contain his curiosity any longer.

"Better than the admiral," answered Riker. "From what I could tell, the ship doesn't seem damaged. But I don't know how long we'll be able to say that, with the hull section in front of us and the saucer section in pursuit."

"Both parts of the *Enterprise?* It's about time." Geordi lifted a hypospray from the case and triggered it. "Hold her still. She may come to with a jolt, and I don't want to hurt her. I'm an engineer, not a doctor."

"Understood." Riker got a firm grip on the admiral's shoulders, and Geordi applied the hypo to her neck.

Nechayev jerked awake and began to groan and struggle. "Whoa, Admiral," cautioned Riker. "You're among friends. Just stay calm. He nodded at Geordi, who scanned the admiral from the neck up. "Sir, you've got a concussion—you need to stay quiet."

The bloody and bruised admiral shifted around in Riker's lap and finally relaxed. After her eyes focused upon him, she managed a weak smile. "If I die now, at least it will be with my fellow officers."

"Well, we're not dead yet," said Geordi, "but we've come close a few times. Maybe we'll get through this alive."

"I don't think so," murmured Nechayev. "I ordered Captain Picard to destroy this saucer, with all aboard."

Geordi looked at Riker. "I see."

"Here," said Riker, moving her head gently. "I stuck a medical probe inside your ear, just like the one I swallowed. That's how Geordi found our coordinates when he beamed us out."

"Leave it in," she said, patting his hand in a surprisingly tender gesture. "I'm glad I'm with the two of you instead of that traitor. And to think, I brought the snake into the nest."

"Don't worry about that now," said Riker, "making mistakes is part of the job."

Nechayev winced. "I forget that sometimes. Look, if you two can beam over to the *Enterprise* and save your lives, do it. But I gave Picard a direct order, and I expect him to carry it out."

"I'm sure he will," said Riker grimly, "but I think we've stopped them—for the moment, anyway."

"Yes, you changed the distress signal. See, I remember some of it." She touched Riker's arm and reached out a trembling hand to Geordi. "Good job. I'll commend you in my report."

With a smile on her battered face, Alynna Nechayev fell asleep in Riker's arms.

Geordi stood up and took his station at the door of the control booth. He dimmed the lights in the vast hangar until it was almost completely dark, and Riker gently set the admiral on the cold floor.

"What are we going to do?" asked Geordi. "Try to get off the ship? If they're slugging it out, I don't figure anybody will drop their shields until it's too late."

Will Riker leaned back against the wall, lifted his knees, and hugged them to his chest. "If I thought we could talk the Maquis into surrendering, I would try. But they're never going to listen to reason—they've proven that over and over again."

"So we wait?" asked Geordi.

Riker looked up. "No, we don't just wait. There may come a moment when we can take over this ship, and we've got to be ready for it, figure out when it will happen."

He stood up and gazed into the dark, empty cavern below them, thinking how well it mirrored his mood. In truth, he didn't know how they could save themselves if Captain Picard was really determined to destroy them. Ironically, to save their lives, they had to root for the enemy to defeat their crewmates. That didn't sound like a strong possibility, so it looked as if destruction was the odds-on favorite.

If Admiral Nechayev was ready to die, and the Maquis were ready to die, that didn't leave much room in between.

Captain Picard stared in amazement at the image on his viewscreen—two identical Galaxy-class saucer sections flying in tandem about a hundred kilometers apart. The hull's sensors were still acting erratically, but they had finally alerted Worf to this remarkable pairing, and Picard had reversed course to investigate. Both saucers seemed to be making for the destination he had guessed, the inhabited planet of Pedrum. If the Maquis tried to break the Prime Directive and land on the planet, Picard knew he would have to go all-out to stop them.

"Neither ship is answering our hail?" he asked Worf.

The Klingon made a low growl. "One of them is jamming all the hailing frequencies, I cannot tell which one it is."

"Ship signatures, life-form readings—anything to distinguish them?"

"No, sir," answered Worf with a frown. "Short-range sensors are still behaving erratically, but my tactical sensors say that both saucers have their shields up."

Picard nodded, tight-lipped. "And you don't need to remind me that our shields are paper thin. Well, this poses an interesting dilemma—two identical ships, one commanded by Doctor Crusher and the other by the enemy. The lady or the tiger?"

"Lady or tiger, sir?"

The captain smiled wistfully. "It's a famous short story. Through various machinations, a young man finds himself confronted by two identical doors. Behind one is the lady of his dreams, whom he may wed if he chooses correctly, and behind the other door is a man-eating tiger. Which does he choose?"

"Yes," Worf asked impatiently, "which one does he choose?"

Picard shrugged and continued to gaze at the viewscreen. "I don't know. The story ends before he makes his decision."

Worf's scowl went all the way up to the ridges on his forehead. "That does not sound like a very satisfying story. It has no ending."

"That's the point, Mr. Worf. It places you in the situation of making the choice. You see, he could also run away and desert the young lady. Not open the door at all."

Worf cleared his throat. "If that were a Klingon story, I know how it would end."

"Oh, yes? How?"

Worf shook his head as if the answer were clear. "He would bravely select a door and throw it open. The tiger would be behind it, and he would fight the tiger to the death. Then his people would mourn him as a great warrior."

Picard smiled slightly and tapped a finger to his chin. "That's a very interesting conclusion. In fact, maybe we should do exactly that."

"Sir?"

"Helm, set course to intercept."

Chapter Twelve

CAPTAIN PICARD CONTINUED TO STUDY the two identical saucers in his viewscreen, wondering if there were an easier way to find out which saucer contained the Maquis. Worf's solution to the lady or the tiger scenario would give him an immediate answer, but not without considerable danger. He tried not to think about Will Riker, Geordi La Forge, and Alynna Nechayev, who might already be dead, for all he knew. They were brave officers, and brave officers were prepared for the worst, although none of them could have imagined they would die at the hands of Captain Picard and the *Enterprise*.

"What exactly is our shield strength?" he asked.

"Fifteen percent," answered Worf. "If we divert

power from impulse engines, we could get another ten or twenty percent."

"Very well," said Picard. "All stop."

"Yes, sir." At the Conn, Ensign Tate carried out the order.

The captain glanced at Worf. "Divert impulse power to shields, then arm phasers."

"Diverting power," said the Klingon. "Shields at thirty-two percent and holding. Arming phasers. What is the target?"

The captain jutted his chin. "Both saucers."

"Including *our* saucer?" asked Worf in amazement.

"Do you know which one is ours?"

"No, sir."

"Then target them both. You said both of them have their shields up, right?"

"Yes, sir."

"Then let's apply the Klingon solution—throw open the door and start fighting. Whichever one is the prototype will think that we have found them out, and they won't know that we fired at *both* saucers. Our enemies are bound to return fire, and I hope Dr. Crusher won't."

"Yes, sir," answered the Klingon, looking pleased at the captain's decision. "Phasers ready."

The captain nodded and tapped his comm badge. "Picard to Data. How soon until we have warp drive?"

"In one minute and forty-seven seconds, sir," answered the android. "We are running diagnostics now."

"Stop running diagnostics," ordered Picard, "and be ready to give me warp drive the moment I ask for it. We're going back into battle."

"Yes, sir," replied the android. "Diagnostics aborted. All indications are that we have reestablished warp drive, but may I suggest a test."

"We'll get one in just a moment. Helm, set a course for Pedrum at warp one."

"Yes, sir. Course laid in."

The captain nodded at the big Klingon. "Fire when ready, Mr. Worf."

"Yes, sir!" The Klingon punched his controls, and phaser beams branched out from the hull section like blazing ripples in a magical pool, engulfing both saucers in pulsating energy. At once, the saucer on the left veered away, and the saucer on the right cut loose with its own phaser weapons.

The battle bridge was jarred by the phaser blast, and Worf staggered to hang on to his console. "Shields down to nine percent!"

"There's your target," said Picard, "fire again!"

As soon as Worf unleashed another phaser attack, which rippled across the bow of the enemy saucer, the captain shouted, "Engage!"

The Maquis returned fire, but their phaser waves found only heat and vapor trails, where the hull section had been a second before vanishing into warp drive.

In the shuttlebay of the prototype saucer, Riker gripped Admiral Nechayev tightly as another round of enemy fire rocked the saucer. She groaned slightly and looked up at him.

"So it begins," she said hoarsely. "The captain is following my orders."

Riker looked up and found Geordi staring at him through his VISOR, as if to say they had never lain down and accepted death easily before. Why should they start now? Riker nodded and gently laid the admiral's head on the deck.

"We'll be right back," he told her. "We've got to get control of the ship. You stay here and don't move."

Even in her weakened state, she glared at him. "Don't do anything to aid the enemy."

"No, sir," answered Riker. He rose to his feet and looked at Geordi with determination, and the two of them marched out of the control booth and down the stairs.

"Where are they?" muttered the big Bajoran, slamming a beefy fist on the Tactical console. "I *know* I had them!"

"They've gone into warp drive," answered Timothy Wiley, slumping dejectedly into the captain's chair. "But at least we know they're too weak to stand and fight, or else they would have. Where is the other saucer section?"

"They've retreated to a hundred thousand kilometers," answered the Ops officer.

Wiley looked down at Henry Fulton, who was sitting cross-legged on the deck like a lonely child. The former commander looked bewildered and shook his head. "I thought for sure jamming the frequencies would confuse them, but I guess not. And we don't even have the admiral anymore."

"Oh, we still have her," said Wiley with disgust, "and her damn orders to destroy us. Helm, resume course to Pedrum, full impulse."

"Yes, sir," answered the officer without much enthusiasm.

"What is our ETA?"

"Approximately fifty minutes."

The young man nodded. "All right, Fulton, it's time you told us everything you know about landing this saucer."

The commander adjusted the brace on his leg and staggered to his feet. "It's entirely automated," he explained. "Essentially, you turn the sensors loose on the planet and pick a likely place to land. What you're looking for is a salt flat, tundra, meadow, beach, someplace level and clear of obstructions. Normally, deep water would be all right, but we don't have anyone to rescue us—so we should stay away from water.

"After you pick the landing site, the computer determines the best orbit and the best deorbital trajectory. Once descent starts, the computer fires impulse engines to slow you down, and it makes all the necessary course corrections. This saucer has the latest forcefields, inertial damping fields, structural integrity fields—everything Starfleet could think to put on a saucer to survive a landing. All we have to do is hang on."

"How many saucer landings have there been?"

"Of a Galaxy-class saucer?" Fulton shrugged. "None."

Wiley tried not to look as worried as he felt.

"What if there's a problem with all these automated systems?"

"Who's the best pilot here?"

The young man with the red mustache looked around and couldn't find a better pilot than himself in this scruffy group. "I guess that would be me."

"Well, then," said Fulton, "get to one of the consoles and familiarize yourself with the procedures. There are several crucial midcourse corrections that need to be made, based on atmospheric conditions."

"All right," said Wiley, rising from his chair and moving toward an unused console. "Linda, start scanning the planet and find us a suitable landing site."

The young woman on the Science station stood erect and answered, "No. The Prime Directive makes sense, and I don't agree with breaking it."

"Then you're relieved," said Fulton sternly. "I'll take over on Science."

Wiley hated to relieve a good officer with one who had proven both egotistical and unbalanced, but he had no choice. Plus, Fulton would know exactly what to look for in a landing site. "Johnson, you are relieved. Get your disruptor and patrol the turbolifts and the transporter rooms. I don't want Riker popping out again and surprising us."

The young woman glared at him for a moment, then drew her disruptor and marched toward the turbolift. Wiley swallowed hard, thinking that he must have sunk pretty low to side with Henry Fulton.

The former Starfleet officer limped to the Science station and sat down. Gazing at the instruments, he cracked his knuckles with satisfaction. "I'm ready."

"Look for a site that's uninhabited," Wiley told him. Fulton gave him an offhand wave.

Feeling sick to his stomach, the young pilot turned to his own console and called up the procedures for an emergency saucer landing. There were approximately five hundred pages to read, and he began scanning through them, looking for the most critical information.

Still, his mind wandered. In one day he had hijacked a Federation ship, kidnapped an admiral, and tried to destroy the *Enterprise,* but those acts paled in comparison to breaking the Prime Directive. In private business dealings, he'd had many opportunities to break the directive for fun and profit, but he'd always resisted. Linda was right—it was the one Federation law that made absolute sense.

The purpose of this entire mission had been to destroy a Cardassian colony, which was a brutal but necessary objective. Now they were potentially destroying an entire culture, pushing it thousands of years into the future. It made him ill to think about it. Whatever notions Timothy Wiley had once held about being a true patriot, misunderstood by the Federation, they would be wiped away by this act. Now he would be a common criminal, even in his own eyes.

* * *

On an identical bridge, Beverly Crusher, Deanna Troi, Guinan, Mason, and Gherink pondered the sight of the runaway saucer plowing across the starscape at full impulse. They were now keeping their distance, after being attacked by their own hull section in what Beverly hoped was a case of mistaken identity. She couldn't blame Jean-Luc, as the saucers were virtually identical, but she had also been attacked by the prototype. Until she was sure what was going on, she was going to keep her distance and keep her shields up. Unfortunately, she didn't have the firepower to stop the prototype, and the hull had mysteriously retreated.

"Has their course changed at all?" she asked.

"No," reported Gherink on Ops. "They are still on course for Pedrum."

"Damn," muttered Beverly, "don't they know it's inhabited?"

"I don't think they care," said Deanna Troi. "Think how desperate they must be—there's no chance of escape without warp drive."

"That's no excuse to ditch a starship on a planet with a primitive society!" Beverly shook her head with disgust. "Who *are* these people?"

"They're Maquis," said Guinan quietly. "I would bet that's who they are. Go easy on them. This is the end of the line—they just don't realize it yet."

"Sir," said Mason on Tactical. "The hull section is hailing us. They're coming out of warp at heading thirty-two mark one hundred."

Beverly put her hands on her hips. "Well, they'd

better not fire at us again. Full stop, but keep our shields up, just in case."

In a blaze of golden streaks, the hull section swooped out of warp drive and came to a stop, its twin nacelles dwarfing the blunted engineering section.

"It's funny-looking without the saucer," said Guinan, expressing everyone's thoughts.

"Captain Picard wishes to speak with the captain," said Mason.

Beverly crossed her arms. "Put him on."

A familiar face appeared on the viewscreen, and Captain Picard looked up from the Ops console with a grin. "Beverly, I can't tell you how glad I am to see you!"

"Glad enough to hold your fire?"

The captain's smile faded. "I can explain all that, but we haven't time. The Maquis have hijacked the prototype and are about to crash-land on Pedrum, which is inhabited by—"

"I know," interjected Beverly. "We have to stop them."

Picard nodded gravely. "I can't stop them alone, and neither can you. Prepare to dock. Let's get the *Enterprise* back in one piece."

Will Riker and Geordi La Forge crouched in the corridor outside the turbolift entrance, wondering what to do next. In the stripped-down saucer, the only controls were on the bridge, and they knew they couldn't storm the bridge. Riker had the disruptor he had taken from the Bajoran, but they were still outgunned six to one. Plus, they didn't know when the next, possibly fatal, attack would come from the *Enterprise*. They had come this far, but now they were stymied.

"All right," whispered Riker, "let's figure out what we really want to do. I think if we could contact the captain, we could beam off this ship."

"Except for the shields," mused Geordi. "We might disable them, but then the saucer would be helpless. Any attack would destroy us. Do we really want that?"

"Only as a last resort. Ideally, we want to take over this ship and surrender it to Captain Picard."

Geordi shrugged doubtfully. "That's a tough order. We could transport to the bridge, but I don't think we can win a shoot-out with one disruptor."

"We've got to lower the odds," agreed Riker. "So why don't we cause some sort of disturbance and *force* them to come after us, then ambush them."

He could tell by the troubled expression on Geordi's face that an ambush wasn't really his idea of a good plan. It wasn't Riker's either, but he was fresh out of good plans.

"All right," said Geordi, "we know we can get into the captain's ready room the same way we got out. I could get their attention and try to escape out the hole. You might be able to pick off a few of them before they see you. In a closed area they can't come after you en masse."

Riker patted his comrade on the back. "Thanks, Geordi. I know this isn't what we want, but we haven't got much choice. Are you up for taking the turbolift? It was working fine when I went to get the admiral."

209

"Sure."

But Geordi hung back nervously as Riker approached the turbolift door, his disruptor drawn and ready. The commander waved his hand in front of the turbolift sensors, knowing the motion would cause the doors to open. Despite his precautions, he really didn't expect to see anyone on the lift, and neither did the young woman who was standing there when the doors opened. They gaped at each other, and she got off the first shot, which skimmed Riker's shoulder and scorched a hole in the bulkhead across from the lift.

Riker staggered backward, nearly losing consciousness from the pain, but he had the sense to toss the disruptor behind him as he fell. The woman rounded the doorway and looked down at him, prepared to finish him off. Upon seeing him wounded and unarmed, she suffered a moment of hesitation, which proved her undoing. Geordi's aim was perfect as his disruptor beam pierced her in the stomach. She sprawled on the deck, and a wisp of smoke rose from the charred hole in her midsection.

"Great," muttered the engineer.

Riker groaned, "You couldn't help it." He struggled to his knees, grabbed the woman's disruptor, and peered into the turbolift. But she had been traveling alone.

"Damn," muttered Geordi. "How old is she, about twenty-three?"

"Can't worry about that now," said Riker with a grunt of pain.

"Hey, it looks like you need the first aid kit."

It was true, thought Riker, even a glancing wound from a Klingon disruptor was impressive. The pain was lessening a bit, but it would still need immediate attention. He had only to look down at the dead woman beside him to know that it could have been far worse. They had cut down the odds as planned, but killing such a brave young woman hadn't brought either one of them any satisfaction. This battle against their own people seemed more insane with every passing moment, and now, in the ultimate act of insanity, they were about to land the saucer on an inhabited planet.

"Next time," said Riker with a grimace, "don't let me volunteer for anything."

"Come on," said Geordi, helping him to his feet. "Our offensive is over for the moment."

The commander pointed down at the lifeless body. "Get her comm badge. We've tried everything else—let's try talking to them again."

Captain Picard strode joyfully upon his own bridge and smiled with great relief at Beverly. "Well done, Captain. Any peculiarities with the new bridge module?"

"No, sir," the doctor answered crisply. She watched Worf, Data, Tate, and several more regular officers file off the turbolift and go to their respective stations. "Are we all relieved?"

"Yes, you are, but only because we know the situation better than you. Feel free to remain as observers." He smiled at Guinan. "If bridge duty appeals to you, I could make you an acting ensign."

"No, thank you," answered Guinan pleasantly. "I don't like the uniforms."

"Very well," said Picard. "Dr. Crusher, have you got full sensors, shields, and communications?"

"Yes, sir."

The captain nodded with satisfaction. "Excellent. And *we* have warp drive. Between the two of us, we're a starship. I hope it's a long time before I have to break up the *Enterprise* again. Data, what is the position of the prototype?"

At blinding speed, the android entered commands on the Ops console. "They are approximately two million kilometers from Pedrum, in standard approach at full impulse."

The captain nodded. "That docking took longer than expected, but we still have time to reach the planet before they do. Helm, set course for Pedrum at warp two."

"Yes, sir," answered Ensign Tate.

"Mr. Worf, we'll drop shields just long enough to fire a brace of four photon torpedoes. Target their primary fusion reactor. We owe it to our comrades to give them a swift death."

"Yes, sir." The Klingon furrowed his head ridges and grunted.

"Wait a minute," said Beverly with alarm, "you mean Will, Geordi, and the admiral are still on that saucer?"

"I'm afraid so," answered Picard, his shoulder slumping. "It isn't my decision, it's a direct order from the admiral."

Deanna leaped to her feet. "Excuse me, sir, isn't there some way we can get them off?"

The captain shook his head sympathetically. "I'm sorry, Counselor. They may already be dead, for all we know. There's no time to delay—we can't let them land that saucer on Pedrum. Helm, is course set?"

"Yes, sir."

"Engage."

Tate pushed a membrane panel, and nothing happened.

"Engage," repeated the captain.

"I'm sorry, sir, but warp engines are not responding."

At the Ops console, Data frowned at his readouts. "Captain, the problem would not appear to lie in the repairs that we made but in a faulty coupler in the new bridge module. As there was no test flight and no attempt to enter warp drive until now, the defect went unnoticed."

Picard gestured helplessly. "Can we fix it?"

The android turned to face him. "Sir, there are two hundred and thirty couplers, and my readouts do not indicate which one is defective. Tricorders may indicate the faulty coupler, but if they do not, we will have to swap them out until we find it."

Through clenched teeth the captain replied, "Get started."

"Yes, sir." The android rose to his feet, strode to the utility cabinet, and took out a tricorder. Then he went to the Conn, dropped to his knees, and flopped over on his back. Tate barely had time to get out of the way as he pried loose the access panel. At once, Worf, Mason, Gherink, and other officers grabbed tricorders and went to work on the other consoles.

Picard shook his head in frustration and turned to Beverly. "Did you request any assistance from Starfleet?"

"No," she answered, "I asked for some advice when I first got here."

"What did they tell you?"

"Proceed with caution."

The captain rubbed his forehead as if he had a terrible headache. "Even if we requested another ship now, it would never get here in time to stop the saucer from landing. By the time we separated the hull section again, it would be too late."

Beverly followed his eyes to the main viewscreen, where an endless field of stars glittered benignly. They both knew there was nothing at all benign about those stars—they brought death, destruction, and sometimes the apple of knowledge to people who weren't prepared to receive it. The price of knowledge was always expulsion from the garden of innocence.

The captain shook his head. "They're going to break the Prime Directive, and there's not a damn thing we can do about it. Heaven help them."

Chapter Thirteen

ON THE PROTOTYPE SAUCER, Timothy Wiley looked over his shoulder at Henry Fulton. The former commander was behaving himself and seemed no longer to care who gave the orders. Wiley's gaze traveled to the Bajoran on Tactical, who was busy diverting power to the shields in anticipation of a last-ditch attack by the *Enterprise*. However, there was no sign anywhere of the hull, saucer, or combined starship; they seemed to have completely lost interest in the escaping Maquis. Wiley shook his head, hardly believing his good fortune.

He turned his attention to the viewscreen and the extraordinary blue-green planet that was quickly filling the frame. It was impossible to look at Pedrum without thinking of Earth, because both planets had the same kind of lush appearance— green continents, sparkling turquoise oceans, swirls of ripe rain clouds. If anything, Pedrum appeared to have even more oceans than earth, fewer continents, and several large islands. Again he looked over his shoulder, expecting someone to tell him that the *Enterprise* was coming out of warp, phasers blasting. But everything on the bridge was calm.

Should they use this moment of calm to make a run for the demilitarized zone? The answer remained the same as the last time he asked himself that—without warp drive, they would be crawling to the DMZ, easy prey for Starfleet. No, it would have to be Pedrum and a new existence, waiting for the day when their comrades from the Maquis would send a rescue party. At least the planet was looking more inviting all the time, and Wiley kept telling himself that they could keep the natives from finding the saucer—if only it weren't as wide as a city block and as tall as a skyscraper.

He frowned. "What is our ETA?"

"Eight minutes," answered the officer on Ops.

"And still no sign of the *Enterprise?*"

"No, sir."

Wiley shrugged, deciding not to look a gift horse in the mouth. "Fulton, have you found a landing site yet?"

"Oh, there's no shortage of those. But your prerequisite that it has to be uninhabited is making the search hard. There aren't any power plants, industries, or clusters of buildings to tell us where the population centers are. I'm picking up scattered life-form readings, but I may not be getting all of them. In other words, I can't guarantee there won't be some people where we land."

"Just do your best." Wiley went back to studying the landing procedures, when suddenly his Bajoran comm badge chimed. He tapped it, figuring it must be Linda. "This is Blue Moon."

"Hello, Blue Moon," responded a deep voice that was definitely not Linda's. "I hate to tell you this, but the young woman is dead."

Wiley bolted upright in his seat. "You bastards!"

"Excuse me," said Riker, "you sent her after us alone, and all we have are these damned disruptors. We had no choice. I'm not calling to brag about that—we have a deal to offer you."

"Don't trust them!" shouted Fulton.

Wiley scowled, thinking how much he would miss Linda, Vylor, and all the other friends he had lost on this misbegotten mission. "Go ahead, but I have to warn you—your precious *Enterprise* is nowhere in sight, and we're landing in seven minutes. I don't know what you have to bargain with."

"This," offered Riker, "if you stay away from that planet, Admiral Nechayev will rescind her order to destroy us."

Now Wiley was forced to smile. "And you'll return us to the DMZ without pressing any sort of charges?"

There was silence for a moment. "You know I can't promise that."

"I have a counteroffer—you come up here and help us land this thing, and I'll let you live."

"All right," said Riker, a little too quickly.

"One more thing." Wiley leaned forward in his chair. "You have two of our disruptor pistols. Before you come up here, I want you to go to a transporter room and beam those weapons to the bridge. Only then will you be allowed to get off the turbolift."

Again there was a pause, and the commander finally replied, "If we beam you the two disruptors, you'll know that we accepted your terms. Riker out."

Will Riker sighed and slumped back against the bulkhead in the control booth that overlooked the empty main shuttlebay. Both Admiral Nechayev and Geordi were gazing expectantly at him, waiting for him to say that he'd been a damn fool to think he could bargain with the Maquis.

He hefted one of the disruptor pistols. "Do these things have anything like a phaser overload, so we could use them as bombs?"

Geordi lifted his disruptor to his VISOR and studied it intently. "Oh, there's an overload setting, all right. The problem is, this thing is so poorly made we couldn't time the explosion." He lowered the weapon and shook his head. "It's just too risky, Commander."

Nechayev struggled to sit up, and there was a little of the old fire in her eyes. "Where is Captain Picard? He never does anything right."

Riker started to say something but then thought better of it. Instead he checked the dressing on his shoulder, which was still throbbing with pain.

There were effective painkillers in the first aid kit, but he was afraid they would knock him out. He was tired enough without getting drugged.

"We've got to stop them," insisted Nechayev. "We can't let them land this saucer on a planet protected by the Prime Directive. The Federation will never be able to correct the damage."

"All right," said Riker resolutely, "I'm going up there and volunteer to land the saucer."

The admiral glared at him, and he held up his hand. "Once I get on the Conn, I'll be in charge of the landing. I can override the computer and bring us down someplace where they'll never find us. Like the bottom of the ocean, or a polar ice cap. If somebody has a better idea, I'm listening."

Geordi and Nechayev looked at each other, but neither spoke up. Finally, Geordi rose to his feet and wiped the dust off his pants.

"Are you staying here, Admiral?" he asked.

"Yes," she answered sullenly. "I'd rather die alone than with traitors like the Maquis."

"Understood," said Riker. He nodded at Geordi, and they headed for the door of the control booth.

"You know, you can seal yourself in here," Geordi told the admiral.

"Don't worry about me," said Nechayev, "just do what you have to do. If you're rescued, tell the truth in your reports. This entire incident was *my* fault."

"Now, Admiral. At least some of the responsibility lies . . ."

"Get going, Commander," she replied wearily.

Riker nodded, wishing he could offer more effective consolation. Geordi opened the door, and they walked down the stairs, across the empty hangar, and out the doors into the corridor. They retraced their steps from a few hours earlier—it seemed like years—to return to the transporter room. Geordi placed the two disruptor pistols on the transporter platform and walked behind the controls.

"I'm going to beam them in front of the command chair," said the engineer. "Tell them to stand clear."

Riker squeezed the comm badge between his fingers and spoke into it. "We're beaming up the disruptors. Stand clear of the command chair."

"All right," answered the man called Blue Moon. "No tricks."

"We're out of tricks," said Riker. "Transporting now." He nodded to Geordi, who plied the controls. A moment later, the disruptors were gone, and they were again unarmed.

"We got them," reported the Maquis leader. "I sincerely hope the two of you have really come to your senses. Survival on this planet is going to be tough, and we could use good people. You never know, it may be possible for Maquis and Federation personnel to get along and work together."

"I doubt it," scowled Riker. He quickly added, "But we'll try."

"Good. Go ahead and transport directly to the bridge. The area in front of the command chair is clear."

The commander nodded to Geordi, who set the transporter controls for a five-second delay. They leaped upon the transporter platform and waited for their molecular patterns to be disassembled, stored in the computer, and rearranged on the main bridge.

Riker wasn't at all surprised to find six disruptor pistols trained upon him and Geordi. He stood patiently, not making any sudden moves. The Maquis seemed to be looking for a reason to shoot him, especially the beefy Bajoran on Tactical.

"What's our status?" he asked, trying to sound like part of the team.

"We're in standard reentry approach," answered the Ops officer. "Orbit will begin in two minutes and start to decay in three point four minutes."

Riker took a cautious step toward the Conn, waiting for someone to get an itchy trigger finger and drill him. When that didn't happen, he said, "If you're going into orbit, you must have picked a landing site."

"A nice, wide beach," said Henry Fulton. "Blue Moon didn't want to disturb the occupants, so we're landing off the beaten path, we think. Where's the admiral?"

"She declined your offer," answered Riker. "I suggest that I take the Conn and La Forge takes Engineering. That's where we'll do the most good."

The man with the red mustache nodded. "Cronin, you stand behind the commander with your disruptor. Don't hesitate to shoot him if he makes any sort of move that endangers this landing. I want to keep my man on Engineering."

"Fine with me," said Geordi. "I'll just sit over here, out of the way."

Riker tried not to show his disappointment at

not having Geordi at the Engineering station. He had counted on his colleague to make it appear as if there was some sort of malfunction that required him to take over. Riker waited patiently until the Maquis officer vacated the Conn, then he took his seat. He studied the readouts, and everything seemed awfully damned normal. In fact, the data stream looked just as it had looked when he was making the approach to Kitjef II, a second before Fulton set off his concussion grenade and plunged them into this nightmare.

"Everything looks in order," he said. He glanced at the viewscreen wondering where the hell the *Enterprise* was. This would be a good time for them to show up. Unfortunately, all he could see was a pristine planet full of people, just waiting to have their entire view of the universe knocked for a loop.

He heard Fulton's snide voice. "You don't really have to do anything, Commander, just let the computer land us. You're there only for insurance, in case something goes wrong."

"All right," said Riker, resting his hands at the sides of the console. "We're going into orbit, but it won't last long. I suggest everyone take a seat. From all the studies I've seen, atmospheric reentry is a rough ride, no matter who's steering the ship."

He was hoping that Cronin and his disruptor would move far enough away that he could manipulate the controls. If anything, the Maquis officer moved closer, and Blue Moon strode to the command chair, sat down, and watched him, too.

Riker took a deep breath and looked at his readouts. "We've entered orbit. Deorbit in thirty seconds, then we enter phase one."

Fulton added with pride, "Prototype modifications are coming on-line. All systems are go."

The next moment they were jarred by what felt like a giant swat. The viewscreen crackled with static and went dark, and the saucer pitched and yawned until it managed to right itself. Riker whirled around to see Cronin stagger to his feet and level his disruptor at him.

"Wait!" he called. "I didn't do it!" While his hands were in the air, another barrage hit them, and Cronin was bounced headfirst into the back of Riker's chair. He rolled over, unconscious; Riker could have easily picked up his fallen disruptor, but he couldn't help staring at his readouts. Then he gawked at the viewscreen as the horizon of Pedrum flattened out and zoomed closer—they were careening out of control into the atmosphere!

"What was that?" yelled Blue Moon.

"Enemy fire," answered the Bajoran. "They must have just come out of warp."

Too little, too late, thought Riker. But at least they had given him a real excuse to take over. "We're off course, in orbital decay!" he declared. "I'm going to manual!"

Before anyone could complain, the saucer began to shake violently, accompanied by structural groaning that made Riker's teeth gnash. The deck turned into a trampoline, and several people got pitched to the floor. Riker was certain they would be torn apart, but the saucer held together long enough for him to make a slight correction, bringing up their nose. It didn't make much difference in their headlong descent through the atmosphere, but it was reassuring that the helm was responding at all.

"SIF, IDF, and forcefields are failing!" cried Fulton. "We're off course—out of control!"

No kidding, Riker felt like saying. "Stop worrying about that and try to get visual back on!"

"Do it!" echoed the acting captain.

They went through another series of jarring vibrations, but the Ops officer stayed glued to his console until he got the viewscreen working again. The heat of the reentry played havoc with the image, but Riker could see the clouds spread below them like islands of sea foam floating on a pale sea. As suddenly as it had begun, the shaking stopped; they speared a cloud bank and were engulfed in opaque mist.

Now atmospheric turbulence shook the craft, and Riker applied himself to his controls, firing thrusters to slow them down and adjust their airflow. He succeeded in leveling their descent, but he was afraid of what he might find in front of him when they emerged from the clouds.

"Fulton!" he shouted. "Is there a landing site around here?"

"There's an island—that's all I see! Mountains! Look out!"

Several Maquis on the bridge gasped when they broke through the clouds and caught sight of two verdant mountains rising in front of them. The tops of the mountains were kissed with snow, and an azure river flowed between them. Riker, however, saw only certain death and wreckage scattered over thousands of kilometers if they hit those peaks. When he caught sight of mud huts surrounding the banks of the river, he edged back on the flaps and tried to get some lift. No doubt about it, this was a Prime Directive disaster in the making!

Riker settled down and tried to pretend that he was sitting at the controls of a very large and obstinate shuttlecraft. He had to *fly* this thing, he told himself, not merely land it. The mountains loomed closer, and he fired every thruster on the starboard side, which succeeded in throwing the saucer into a crude bank. He watched the mountains curl under the belly of the saucer, and he didn't want to think how close they had come to smashing into them.

As they leveled out, Riker could see the shimmering blue horizon, and he realized that he was indeed looking at a large island. Where there was an island, there was water, lots of water.

"I found a beach!" shouted Fulton. "It's not as good as the first one, but it will do."

"Send me the coordinates," said Riker. He had no intention of landing the saucer on a beach, not when this island was so clearly inhabited. There was another variable—the *Enterprise.* Since the captain had fired at them, it meant they had to be in orbit. He could crash the saucer into the ocean with some hope of all of them being beamed off.

Riker made that his goal and lifted the nose of the saucer a little higher in order to glide beyond the coastline.

"Hey!" shouted Fulton. "You're not headed toward the beach!"

Riker held his hands high in the air. "You want to take over? Be my guest."

"No, no, keep flying!" ordered Blue Moon. "Fulton, just do what he tells you!"

Before Riker could get his hands down, they plunged into a driving thunderstorm. Lightning rippled across their bow, and the deck dropped out from under them. No matter how frantically Riker plied the controls, they kept losing altitude. On the viewscreen he saw vast wetlands stretching beneath them, broken up by occasional villages and agricultural plots. With every second, the shallow swamp loomed closer, and that was definitely *not* where he wanted to come down.

In desperation, he fired the impulse engines, and the saucer bucked like a bronco at the rodeo. Everyone, including Riker, was tossed to the deck, and the saucer shot straight up for several seconds like a pancake. With a terrible groaning sound, the saucer stopped its ascent and hovered above the rain clouds, then it plunged into a monstrous belly dive.

The commander crawled back into his seat, hardly cognizant of the moaning and wounded people around him. He pulled back every flap and fired every thruster to try to pull them out of their nosedive, but he only succeeded in putting them into a deadly spiral. Instead of fighting the spiral, he banked the saucer into it, and they made gradually wider circles until they swooped out of the dive, skimming the tops of the trees beneath them.

The saucer had practically no altitude now, and it was all he could do to keep the nose up until he could get over the ocean. But he had to find the ocean first! As Riker stared at the viewscreen, he felt the cold metal of a Klingon disruptor at the base of his neck.

"I know what you're doing," said Henry Fulton. "It won't work. Set her down *now!*"

From the corner of his eye, Riker could see Geordi lying on the deck, apparently unconscious. But there was no way to tell if Geordi was watching them through his VISOR until saw the engineer lift a finger in what looked like a signal. The other Maquis seemed to be unconscious or immobilized by wounds, so Fulton was the only threat. Riker banked sharply, making the commander stagger to his left and land on his bad leg. When he started to stumble, Geordi sprang to his feet and rushed the man, catching his gun hand before he could turn around.

The two men battled over the disruptor weapon, sending a stray beam streaking into the viewscreen. It exploded, showering them with shards of phosphorescent crystal. Geordi and Fulton scrambled around in the glassy debris, both of them trying to gain the upper hand, and Geordi finally twisted Fulton's wrist until he screamed with pain and dropped the disruptor. Then the engineer smashed

Fulton in the jaw with a hard jab, and he crumpled to the floor, unconscious. Breathing heavily, Geordi picked up Fulton's disruptor.

It was a Pyrrhic victory at best, because now they were flying blind, almost scraping the ground. Geordi whirled around and leveled his weapon at someone else, and Riker turned to see Blue Moon aiming his own disruptor.

"Don't fire!" shouted Riker. "If you want to die, just wait a second."

The red-haired man rubbed his head. "What can I do to help?"

"Get on Science—find the direction of the ocean."

Blue Moon stared at him, gripping his weapon nervously. He obviously realized that Riker did not intend to land the saucer but to sink it in the ocean. The young man looked around and saw that all of his fellow Maquis were either dazed or unconscious. With a look of relief on his face, Blue Moon holstered his weapon and limped to the Science console. Geordi took over on Ops.

"All right," said Blue Moon, "you're close, but you want to bear two hundred eighty degrees azimuth."

Riker made the course correction. "Thank you. I'd like to promise you some kind of leniency, but I don't think I can make any promises at the moment."

"Understood," said the Maquis leader. "I really prefer to die with a clear conscience."

Out of habit, Riker looked up to where there was normally a viewscreen, but there was nothing left of it but scorched circuitry and dangling particles of laminated crystal. He tried to keep the nose of the saucer up, but gravity had them in its inexorable grip.

"We've cleared the coast," said Blue Moon, "but we need deeper water."

Riker shook his head as he entered futile commands. "We'll have to take whatever we get—I've got nothing left."

He braced himself for impact, but it didn't come as quickly as he expected. As a few more seconds passed, the commander began to breathe easier, thinking they were well over the ocean now.

"Okay," reported the Maquis officer, "we've got a depth of two kilometers."

"And an altitude of one meter," added Geordi.

Riker braced himself as the saucer struck the choppy seas with such force that it shot a mammoth wall of water hundreds of meters into the air. Then the saucer skipped upon the ocean like a flat stone, tossing all three men out of their seats. Riker sprawled on the deck and hung on to the base of his chair as the saucer section became the galaxy's biggest speedboat.

After what seemed like an eternity, the giant saucer came to a stop and bobbed in the water, and the planet of Pedrum had a gleaming, new island.

Dazed, hardly believing that they had survived such a wild reentry, Riker rolled over and muttered, "Whoa, I hope we never have to go through that again."

"I can't imagine we will," said Geordi in agreement.

The commander dragged himself to his knees. "Before we blow the hatches and sink this thing, let's see if we can contact the *Enterprise*. They must be in orbit."

"I'll do it." Geordi limped up the ramp behind the command chair, stepped over the unconscious body of the Bajoran, and took his place at the Tactical station. He entered some commands, waited a few seconds, then frowned. "They're not responding. I'll try a distress signal."

Another minute passed, and Geordi continued to glower at the instruments. "I don't get it—they're not responding."

"Well, *somebody* shot us down," grumbled Riker. "Maybe the radio is done for. I'd be surprised if anything still worked after that."

"Listen," said the man called Blue Moon, "I helped you ditch this saucer far away from the settlements, so you owe me one. Could you transport my people ashore before you sink it? Is it necessary we all die?"

Riker looked back at Geordi, and the engineer shrugged. "If the transporters are still working, we could all beam back over the island, but how is the *Enterprise* going to find us?"

"There must be some emergency beacons around here somewhere." Riker got up to check the utility cabinet when he heard a groan, and he turned to see the big Bajoran coming slowly back to consciousness. Riker quickly picked up a fallen disruptor, and Geordi leveled his weapon and backed away. The Bajoran blinked angrily at them and reached for the disruptor in his holster.

"Hold it!" ordered Blue Moon, aiming his disruptor at his fellow Maquis. "There will be no more fighting—we're all in the same boat, literally. Commander Riker got us down in one piece, as promised, and he's going to beam us over to dry land before he sinks the saucer. Aren't you, Commander?"

Before Riker could answer, a very peculiar thing happened. Four shimmering transporter columns appeared in the center of the bridge and began to materialize into humanoid shapes. With great relief, Riker lowered his disruptor, thinking for sure it was a rescue party from the *Enterprise*. After all that insanity, it appeared as if they had managed to protect Pedrum from a Prime Directive violation and be saved in the bargain. *All's well that ends well,* he thought to himself.

Only the four figures that materialized on the bridge of the prototype saucer were not humans or Starfleet officers.

"Cardassians!" bellowed the Bajoran, jumping up and cutting loose with disruptor fire.

He sliced one of the wiry Cardassians completely in half, but the other three directed their weapons at him and turned his chest into a glowing ball of flame. Shrieking insanely and shooting wildly, the Bajoran staggered down the platform, and the Cardassians kept firing at him, which gave Riker, Geordi, and Blue Moon plenty of time to aim and fire back.

A second later, all four Cardassians lay dead, their corpses smoldering and their black eyes staring up from thick, bony eye sockets.

Chapter Fourteen

Geordi shook his head in amazement and stared at the four dead Cardassians. "How the hell did *they* know to come *here?*"

The man called Blue Moon looked ashen. "I sent a signal back to the DMZ. It was *encrypted!*"

"I'd say you need a new algorithm," replied Geordi.

Riker grabbed the unconscious Henry Fulton and began dragging him to the turbolift. "Come on! Get everybody out of here! They weren't expecting the bridge crew to be armed to the teeth, and who knows what they'll do next."

There were three wounded Maquis, and Riker, Geordi, and Blue Moon grabbed them and dragged them into the turbolift with Fulton. They heard devices on the dead Cardassians start to beep, and Riker rushed from body to body, plucking the gadgets from their utility belts. He hurled the devices into a corner just a fraction of a second before they disappeared in a shimmering transporter beam.

Riker caught his breath, but the respite didn't last long as the communications panel on the Tactical console started to chime.

"They're hailing us," said Geordi.

"Yeah, I know." Riker looked grimly at the console. "I'll try to stall them. Get the wounded down to transporter room three and let me know if the transporters are still working. If they are, I'll blow the hatches."

"What about the admiral?" asked Geordi.

"I'll get her."

Geordi and Blue Moon piled into the turbolift with the wounded Maquis, and the doors shut, leaving Riker alone on the bridge—alone except for several dead bodies. He walked to the Tactical station and started to put the Cardassian hail on visual before realizing he didn't have that option, so he put it on audio.

"Come in, disabled vessel," demanded an angry voice, "this is Gul Duvest of the Cardassian starship *Grosvak*. I demand to speak to my diplomatic team!"

"This is Commander Riker, captain of a Federation prototype vessel. I would hardly call the people you beamed down—without permission—a diplomatic team."

"And I would hardly call you a Federation

vessel. We know you are Maquis—we intercepted your message, and we raided your command post on New Hope. We know all about your plans to brutally attack our civilian colony. Now, I demand to speak to my team, or we will open fire. Where are they?"

Riker looked at the dead bodies sprawled in front of the smashed viewscreen. "They're here, and they're not going anywhere. I assure you, Gul Duvest, I am a Federation officer, and we have thwarted the plans of the Maquis. So there is no need for your interference."

"If you have thwarted them, then you must have Maquis prisoners. Do you have the terrorists called Peacock and Blue Moon?"

Riker paused, trying to think of the least harmful lie. "Blue Moon is dead. Peacock is our business."

"Yes, I know," said the Cardassian snidely. "A Starfleet officer, isn't he? How embarrassing. You have five seconds to let me speak to my team, or we will open fire."

"You can't do much harm to this vessel," said Riker, trying to keep stalling. "We were about ready to blow the hatches and sink it. How did you get here so quickly?"

"We are a diplomatic ship," growled the Cardassian, "en route to a peace conference. But we were diverted to attend to this matter. Now, let me speak to my men!"

"I'll have them brought up here." Riker flicked off communications and started tugging nervously on his beard. *Come on, Geordi, where are you?*

The communications panel chimed at the same

instant that the Bajoran comm badge in his pocket beeped. With relief, he pulled the badge out of his pocket and squeezed it. "Riker here."

"It's La Forge. The transporter is working, but we're losing power. We need to beam off right now, if we're going to. I've picked what I think is a deserted stretch of beach, but Fulton and some of these Maquis may be a handful to control."

"Just get them over there—we'll round them up later. Leave the coordinates on the transporter, and I'll get the admiral. Riker out."

He tooked a deep breath and answered the insistent hail. "This is Commander Riker of the Starfleet prototype vessel."

"I know!" screeched the Cardassian Gul. "You are trying my patience—I demand to speak to my people right now."

"They're on their way," answered Riker. He dashed to the Ops station and glanced at the readouts, noting with satisfaction that the transporter was moving bodies off the ship. Unfortunately, he didn't think the escape would go unnoticed on the Cardassian sensors.

It didn't. "You're abandoning ship!" yelled the voice. "Now you really *do* have only five seconds before I open fire!"

Well, thought Riker, it would save him the trouble of scuttling the saucer. He started into the turbolift but realized that he didn't want to be trapped inside there when all hell broke loose, so he dashed into the captain's ready room. He was crawling through the hole in the panel that he had kicked open earlier when a Cardassian compressor beam struck the saucer. Riker couldn't see the beam go straight through the observation lounge, eat up fifteen decks, and shoot out the underbelly, but he felt the monstrous shock wave it produced.

The saucer bounced on the water like a toy boat. If Riker hadn't been in such an enclosed space, he would have been killed, but he only bounced around the access space and picked up more bruises. When his head cleared, he heard the ceiling of the bridge come crashing down behind him, and he dove headfirst into the Jeffries tube.

Riker hung on the ladder in the Jeffries tube, and he heard an awful groan—then the saucer tilted dramatically and sent him swaying over the vertical drop. He kept thinking the ship would right itself, but then he remembered they weren't in space but in water; and the saucer was picking up tons of water every second. Riker knew he had to get moving if he was going to rescue the admiral. Fortunately, the main shuttlebay was only a couple decks below the bridge, so he didn't hurry as he picked his way down the radically tilted ladder.

Then he heard a strange sound, like a *whoosh* of air, only it wasn't air. The noise swiftly turned into a roar, and with horror, Riker looked down to see a wall of black water come racing up the Jeffries tube. He scampered down rung after rung, trying to race the water to the access tube on the deck below.

The saucer groaned and shifted again, and his legs swung out over the rushing water. The deafening noise made him feel that he was trapped inside a giant drainpipe. In desperation, Riker swung down to the first exit he could find, a horizontal tunnel that was now slanting upward at a bizarre angle. He knew there had to be a bulkhead hatch at the other end of the tube, and he scrambled on bleeding hands and knees to escape the surging water. The spray alone was freezing, and frigid water lapped at his heels as he reached the hatch.

Frantically, he pushed it open and was about to tumble into the corridor when something grabbed his leg. Riker whirled around to see a large, black tentacle clawing its way up his leg, and he screamed. More tentacles lashed out, feeling for a hold in the slick tunnel, and an unspeakably slimy beast oozed its way out of the swirling water. Riker fumbled for his disruptor, finally drew it, and blew a hole in the creature, splattering gobs of flesh all over the inside of the tunnel. The bloody thing slipped back into the water, and Riker hurtled through the hatch.

Panting with terror, he shut and bolted the hatch behind him. Before he could catch his breath, there was another monstrous explosion; ten meters away from him, the corridor disappeared to be replaced by blinding daylight. The saucer shifted again and tossed him away from the daylight, and he went sliding on his back down the slippery corridor, straight toward a maelstrom of brackish water fifty meters away.

Riker clutched his disruptor, wondering whether he should use it on himself as an alternative to drowning, or worse. Then he saw a turbolift door on his right, and he stuck his foot out to stop his slide as he grabbed the door with his free hand. Frigid water swirled up his legs, numbing them instantly, but he kept the disruptor dry and blasted a trench in the deck. With relief, he watched most of the water cascade into a lower deck, but his eyes caught something black just before it leaped out of the water. He fired the disruptor and caught a giant eel-like fish in the head. Its snapping jaws fell at his feet while its tail kept thrashing all the way into the trench.

The encounter spurred him into motion, and he quickly realized that the daylight at the end of the corridor was his only hope. With short bursts of the disruptor, he blasted holes in the corridor at intervals to use as handholds and steps. Then he dragged himself out of the water and began to climb toward daylight.

After an arduous climb upon legs that were devoid of feeling, Will Riker reached a jagged hole where there had once been a corridor and staterooms. Now there was sunlight, a bracing sea breeze, and a salty mist that smelled intoxicating. If this had to be the last sensation he ever knew, then he would take it. Groaning with exhaustion, he hauled himself over the charred remains of the hull and soon found himself where no one had ever been before—standing atop a Galaxy-class starship as it sank into the ocean. The sky was glorious, filled with birds coming to see the excitement.

Only about ten percent of the saucer remained above the waves, he figured, but the sinking had slowed a bit. There were probably enough sealed compartments and air pockets to keep the craft afloat for hours or seconds—it was impossible to tell. He sat on top of a sensor housing and gazed in awe at the primordial sea of a primitive planet. Riker had tasted death more often than most, but he had never imagined *this* as his final fate. Being vaporized, sucked into space, suffocating—those were the deaths he imagined in his line of duty. Instead, he was going to die as his predecessors had died a millennium ago, in the cold grip of Neptune. Admiral Nechayev had probably already gone that route.

In a million years, he wondered, would the seas of Pedrum recede, affording Pedrian archeologists a chance to make a remarkable discovery? Maybe in a couple thousand years they would have submarines and bathyscaphes to scour the ocean floor, and they would find the saucer but have to leave it to the barnacles and gilled creatures. He hoped they would be able to cope with the discovery, whenever it occurred.

At any rate, he had postponed that day for a long, long time.

Geordi staggered a few steps in soggy black sand before plunging up to mid-thigh and realizing that he, and the Maquis with him, were in serious trouble. What he had mistaken for a beach was really a quagmire of quicksand on the edge of a stagnant bay. The very air of the island seemed humid and oppressive, and the insects had started to swarm around the helpless survivors. In more ways than one, it felt as if they were being sucked into the planet, and Geordi had the irrational fear that Henry Fulton would get what he wanted— they would live but never be rescued.

He heard shouts, and he whirled around to find that Fulton, Blue Moon, and the other Maquis were panicking and dropping the wounded into the quicksand. Fulton stumbled, went under, and came up spitting out globs of sand that looked like caviar. The more they struggled, the deeper they sank and the louder they wailed. If there was anyone around, thought Geordi with annoyance, they had been duly alerted by now.

"Don't panic!" he snapped at them. Geordi pointed to a wounded Maquis woman. "Turn her over onto her back, stretch her out, and let's see what happens."

After they turned the unconscious woman onto her back, she floated atop the tar-black quicksand, breathing easily. The sand covered her blond hair and turned it black, but it kept her upright. One by one, the Maquis stopped struggling and began to float, crawl, and paddle themselves through the muck. Only two Maquis couldn't walk, and they were dragged on their backs through the grime.

Geordi made for the wispy trees waving in the distance, behind a ridge of tall, windblown grasses. He began to think of all the things they needed but didn't have for a survival mission, such as water and food. They had plenty of weapons, but the disruptors weren't exactly hunting weapons, unless you preferred your food incinerated. In due time, the weapons would be out of charge with no way to recharge them.

When Commander Riker showed up, they would have a beacon, maybe, and Admiral Nechayev. Geordi stopped to peer over his shoulder at the vast, soggy beach behind him, and he admitted to himself that Will Riker was not coming. Even kilometers away, they had heard the explosion and didn't have to think too deeply about what it was.

Geordi squinted into the sunny glare and thought he saw something solid and cool through his VISOR. He reached into the goo, and his hand struck a root, the first indication that he was getting to firmer soil. Following a trail of roots, he finally dragged himself out of the sand and staggered forward, sloshing up to his ankles. The others, seeing him walking, quickened their pace and soon dragged themselves out of the bog. After making the wounded comfortable, they collapsed where they lay; it was hard to tell them apart from the muck they were covered with.

Fulton lifted his disruptor and aimed it at Geordi's back.

"Put that down," breathed Blue Moon. "You damned idiot."

The grimy commander turned the weapon on his fellow Maquis. "My plan was *perfect!* You ruined it, you and him!"

"Your plan was always risky," countered Blue Moon, "but it was worth a try."

Fulton snarled like a trapped ferret. "Yes, and I ruined my career because you didn't have the guts to do what had to be done!"

Geordi almost told the traitor to shut up, but then he remembered that he was waving a disruptor around. As long as these short-tempered firebrands were all armed to the teeth, he couldn't exactly speak his mind. He was the enemy, and he could quickly find himself a prisoner or worse. Perhaps the wisest course was to put some space between himself and the bickering Maquis, thought Geordi as he started to edge away.

"You ruined the perfect plan!" shouted Fulton, aiming the disruptor at him again.

Geordi turned sideways to present less of a target, and he felt the ground with his toe, deciding it was firm enough to run on. "You know," he said, trying to sound calm, "you're alive, and that's more than we can say about some people. I'm going to scout ahead."

Then he started running.

"He's escaping!" yelled Fulton, jumping to his feet.

"Don't shoot!" he heard one of them yell, and he sprawled into a gully as a disruptor beam streaked over his head and scorched a sand hill behind him.

He drew his own weapon and waited, but all he heard were angry shouts. Cautiously, Geordi rose up enough to see that Fulton had been subdued by his own comrades, so he got into a crouch and dashed toward the forest, paying no heed to the calls from Blue Moon and the others to come back. He'd had enough of the Maquis for one day.

Leaping over roots and tree trunks, Geordi bounded into the succulent underbrush and dropped behind a row of leaves the size of elephant ears. Despite his exhaustion, every nerve was on end, and his muscles kept twitching involuntarily. It wasn't just the Maquis making him nervous. It was also the humidity, the bugs, the whole charged atmosphere of the island. The sensations were all so intense that he felt as if he were hallucinating.

After several minutes, he could still see the Maquis on the beach, arguing among themselves, too weary and disheartened to chase after him. He heard a twig snap, and he whirled around to see a hulking figure standing directly behind him, poised to spear him with an iron lance that had to be four meters long. The humanoid was covered with coarse brown hair over his entire body, and it twisted into a mane that grew up his back and over the top of his skull. Hair grew all over his porcine face, but it was his huge, curled tusks that commanded Geordi's attention. He kicked the human's leg with a hooved foot and snorted.

Geordi wanted to disappear, but that was not an option. The last thing he wanted was to draw his disruptor and have to kill a primitive who had done nothing to deserve this untimely invasion of his home. Still, the drive for self-preservation was a strong one, and Geordi found that he could not simply lie there and die. His grimy fingers slipped around the butt of the disruptor, and he told himself he would shoot at the lance itself, and only the lance. His muscles tensed; he was ready to roll away and come up shooting.

Then he and the Pedrian were both startled by the sound of voices in the humid forest. The Pedrian stared at him, then in the direction of the voices, then at the Maquis on the beach, and grunted unhappily. He dropped to his haunches and stuck his spear point under Geordi's throat;

the human gulped and held perfectly still. Against all odds, he was still alive, and there was no reason not to wait and see if his luck would hold another few seconds.

The Pedrian was staring into the forest, and Geordi shifted slightly to see what he was looking at. They both hunkered down at the sight of a dozen armed Cardassians moving stealthily through the forest, about fifty meters away. They hadn't spotted Geordi and his new acquaintance, but they had clearly spotted the noisy group of survivors on the beach and were moving steadily toward them.

The Pedrian wrinkled his boarlike snout, clicking his tusks together in the process. He stared from Geordi to these new intruders, looking like a child trying to make up his mind between two unappetizing vegetables on his dinner plate. Geordi realized that he had to do something in the next few seconds, or the Maquis on the beach were going to be massacred. However, any sudden move could bring withering fire down upon him and the unlucky Pedrian.

Very slowly, Geordi reached up and touched his VISOR. He felt the spear point dig deeper into his chin, but he tried to ignore it as he calmly removed his VISOR and stared at the Pedrian with opaque, sightless eyes. Geordi had never seen his own eyes, of course, but he had heard the occasional gasps when removing his VISOR; so he assumed they were rather startling. He heard a frightened mumble, followed by a thud as the lance hit ground. Then he heard the padding of bare feet. Geordi sprawled into the bushes and held perfectly still, hoping the Cardassians hadn't seen the Pedrian's sudden departure.

Unfortunately, he heard voices, followed by a pair of footsteps coming closer. Geordi hurriedly pushed the VISOR back onto his face and felt around on the ground for the spear. Cardassians thrived in heat like this, and he had no chance of escaping from them when he could hardly breathe. His only hope of escape was to make them think he wasn't threatening, so he crawled to his knees and threw the spear as far as he could in the general direction of the Cardassians.

He scurried away under some gigantic leaves and kept crawling until he heard the Cardassians' laughter. They had found the spear and had obviously decided that its owner was not a threat. Gulping the humid air, Geordi spun around on his stomach and watched the two invaders return to their squad. Gaunt and leathery, the Cardassians moved through the primordial forest like raptors on the stalk.

With sweat, sand, and insects in every fold of his body, Geordi got into a crouch and trudged through the forest. He wasn't thinking clearly, and his legs had decided on their own to churn, putting as much distance as possible between himself and the Cardassians. He knew he had to warn the Maquis, but he had a difficult time forcing himself back to the beach. They had killed his friends, tried to kill *him*—every instinct in his body screamed at him that they were the enemy! At the very least, it was every man for himself.

Acting against his baser instincts, Geordi stopped in the forest, heaved a disgusted sigh, and took a right turn toward the sound of the crashing ocean.

More than once, he thought he heard something, and he crouched down to listen and gaze around the sticky, dripping forest. When neither Cardassians nor Pedrians jumped out of the underbrush, he went back to jogging toward the beach, trying not to trip on the numerous roots and vines that littered the forest floor.

Geordi crawled to the last row of plants on the edge of the forest, leaned on his elbows, and gazed across the still bay. Through his VISOR he tried to pick out the Maquis party from among the grassy, black dunes, but he was too weary to concentrate. He finally closed his eyes and listened. Soon the hot breeze brought the sound of bickering voices, demoralized and beaten, and he opened his eyes and stared at the bobbing of heads just visible past a windblown ridge of sand.

If only he had some way to warn them without tipping off the Cardassians, too, but he had lost his communicator badge long ago. Except for lung power, he couldn't think of any way to deliver the news.

Reluctantly, Geordi jumped to his feet and shouted, "Cardassians in the forest! Cardassians! Take cover!"

The Maquis' survival instincts were well-honed, and they dove to the sand without questioning the source of the warning. A moment later, the Cardassians unleashed their handheld compressor beams, which wavered across the sand dunes like heat mirages. Chunks of beach exploded from within, showering the air with black dust, but the Maquis leaped to their feet and used the dust cover to return fire. The Cardassian front line was cut in half by the deadly disruptor beams, and trees and bushes burned like the fires of perdition behind them.

For several awful moments, the combatants stood their ground and fired at one another, oblivious to their comrades who fell beside them. But the Cardassians had the numbers and better cover in the forest, and they reduced the black beach to what looked like an arid moon full of craters, devoid of life. The Maquis soon stopped returning fire and lay still. One by one, four surviving Cardassians staggered out of the forest and looked dazedly at one other. Then they leveled their weapons and marched toward the bodies.

Geordi gaped in stunned sorrow at the devastation. He wouldn't have thought that anything could have lived through that firestorm until he heard a meek voice yelling, "I surrender! I surrender!"

He saw a white T-shirt being waved desperately above a dune that was well behind the front line of Maquis dead, and he heard the voice again. "I'm a Starfleet officer! Spare me! I surrender!"

"Stand up!" growled one of the Cardassians, waving his rifle in a no-nonsense manner. "Hands above your head!"

Geordi leveled his disruptor and nearly blasted Henry Fulton himself when he saw the traitor slide down a dune with his hands over his head. Two

Cardassians promptly grabbed him, tossed him facedown in the sand, and frisked him. The other two made half-hearted advances toward Geordi's position, knowing the warning had to have come from somewhere, but the fight had been burned out of them. They finally regrouped, sat Fulton upright, and communicated with their ship.

A few seconds later, all of the Cardassians—dead, alive, and wounded—vanished in the shimmering haze of transporter beams. Henry Fulton went with them.

Chapter Fifteen

"SIR," SAID DATA TO THE CAPTAIN, "there is a Cardassian Galor-class warship orbiting the planet of Pedrum."

Captain Picard frowned, wondering what else could happen to them on this blasted mission. Finally, having found the faulty coupler in the new bridge module, they had repaired the warp drive and arrived at Pedrum, not knowing whether the saucer had attempted a landing or not. But the presence of a large vessel, even a Cardassian one, meant that something had happened. Perhaps a rescue, perhaps an attack.

"What is our ETA, Mr. Data?"

"Two minutes until standard orbit."

The captain nodded and looked back at Lieutenant Worf. "Open a hailing channel. I'll speak to them."

The Klingon worked his console. "Hailing channel open."

Picard jutted his jaw and pulled down his tunic. "Cardassian vessel, this is Captain Picard of the starship *Enterprise*. This is Federation space, and you are orbiting a planet that is protected by the Prime Directive, which forbids contact with them in any form. I trust you have a very good reason for this incursion."

A smiling Cardassian Gul came on the viewscreen, looking like the soul of conciliation. "Captain Picard, I assure you we meant no incursion. I am Gul Awarkin of the *Taranor* and we were on our way to the peace conference on Pacifica when our sensors picked up a ship in distress. Are you aware that a large Federation vessel has crash-landed on this planet? It's sinking into the ocean as we speak."

Picard stepped forward. "Did you effect any rescues?"

"Not yet," the Cardassian answered forlornly. "But we can send you the coordinates of the wrecked ship. I believe there is at least one life-sign reading on the ship."

"Yes, send coordinates," answered Picard. He looked expectantly at Worf, and the Klingon nodded once the data started coming in. "Helm, alter orbit to take us there."

"Yes, sir," said Tate on the Conn.

Commander Data studied his readouts and reported, "I have located the saucer section. Eighty-six percent of the saucer is underwater, and there are massive breaches in the hull. There is one life-form clinging to the surface of the saucer."

"Which transporter room is staffed?"

"Number three, sir. Sending coordinates."

"Transporter room three," ordered Picard, "lock on to the life-form reading at these coordinates. Transport as soon as you have a lock."

"Yes, sir," answered Mendez, "I anticipate another thirty seconds."

"I'm on my way," said Beverly Crusher, heading toward the turbolift. Deanna Troi was right behind her.

"I'm with you!" called Guinan, gliding after them.

"Excuse me, Captain," said the cultured voice of the Cardassian Gul. "You appear to have matters well in hand—may we leave now?"

"You are a long way from Pacifica—I find it hard to believe you were just cruising by."

"We are late, Captain Picard," said the Gul, dropping the pretense of pleasantry. "Needless to say, we have a common enemy, and we are only too glad to see them fail. I'm relieved that our presence was not really necessary here. As you humans say, 'All's well that ends well.'"

Picard crossed his arms. "I'm not sure this has ended well. If there are any irregularities, your government will hear from me. But thank you for your assistance."

The Cardassian sneered. "Ah, that famous Federation gratitude. You are most welcome, Captain. Until next time."

With that, the viewscreen went dark, followed by a glimpse of the Cardassian warship. Colored mustard and brown, its shape reminded Picard of a hammerhead shark he had seen in the West Indies. It had the same kind of deadly leanness as it came about gracefully and cruised out of orbit.

An amazed and delighted voice broke in, "Captain, I've got him! It's Commander Riker!"

The captain broke into a broad smile and nodded at Worf and the rest of the bridge crew. "Well, that is good news! Can you lock onto any other life-signs? Or comm badges?"

"Negative," came the reply. "Dead bodies perhaps, sealife, but nothing definite. No comm badges."

Data concurred. "Our sensors are having difficulty piercing the seawater, which has an extremely high magnesium content. I am attempting to adjust for it now."

The captain nodded gravely. "Keep looking. Everyone, keep looking."

When Deanna Troi saw Will Riker sprawled on the floor of the transporter room—looking as if he'd been chewed, swallowed, and spit out by a whale—she nearly bolted past Beverly Crusher to get to him. But she remembered her place and hung back as Beverly opened her medical tricorder and gave him a quick examination. He gazed gratefully at all of them and even gave her a slight smile, but he seemed dazed. She could feels waves of anxiety oozing out of him, and she just gave him a thumbs-up and smiled encouragingly.

"Wow!" said Guinan. "You didn't look this bad after your last shore leave."

"This is the worst shore leave I've ever had," he wheezed in agreement.

"Don't talk or move," ordered Beverly. "No, serious injuries but lots of little ones, including dehydration. The worst is that disruptor burn. And how is it that you have a medical probe inside you?"

Riker bolted upright and stared at them like a wild man. "Medical probe! Have you got the admiral yet?"

Beverly pushed him back down. "Don't worry about the admiral."

"No!" he rasped, gripping her arm. "Admiral Nechayev has this same medical probe inside her! See if you can find it and lock on."

Beverly rose to her feet, strode across the transporter room, and handed her tricorder to the operator. Deanna took that opportunity to sit beside Will and give him a hug. To her surprise, he was shivering.

"Damn cold water," he breathed. "Damn cold."

"All right," called Beverly, "we've locked on. Transporting."

"She could be dead," Riker whispered to Deanna, as if trying to prepare her for a gruesome sight.

On the transporter pad a glimmering column of light materialized into a lumpen, shivering ball. Guinan and the doctor rushed to Admiral Nechayev, who was curled in a fetal position, staring straight ahead. Like Will, Alynna Nechayev appeared to have been beaten and traumatized and was hanging on to sanity by a thin thread. Unlike Will, her clothes were at least dry.

As Guinan held her hand, Nechayev seemed to focus her dazed eyes upon Riker. She croaked, "It's about time."

He nodded, holding Deanna a little tighter. "Yes, it is. You sealed yourself inside the control booth?"

The admiral nodded, her eyes growing huge, as if seeing an apparition. "The entire shuttlebay filled up—with sea monsters!"

"I know," said Riker, shivering. "I know."

"That's enough discussion," ordered Dr. Crusher. "If I had my full staff, both of you would be in isolation by now. Guinan, would you care to find a food slot and serve these two some warm apple cider."

"Aye, sir," said Guinan, gliding into the corridor.

"What became of La Forge?" asked the admiral.

The commander shook his head. "He got off the ship with the Maquis."

"The next one who speaks gets a court-martial," warned Beverly. "If you lived, maybe Geordi did, too. So let's try to think good thoughts. I'm going to go get you some blankets and enlist some help getting you moved. I'll be right back."

Riker nodded and closed his eyes. To Deanna he

whispered, "Geordi will be all right—if he can get away from them."

Lieutenant Commander La Forge looked down at the blasted bodies of the Maquis. He couldn't look at any of the bodies for long because of the thorough job the Cardassian compressor beams had done on them. And what had they died for? The chance to fight and die on another day—that was all that awaited them even if their mad plan had succeeded. It was insane.

He stopped to look down at Blue Moon, whose red hair and mustache paled beside the redness of his blood, which oozed into the black sand and made a brown pool. Suddenly Blue Moon's eyes blinked open, and his chest heaved with a hollow, rattling sound.

Geordi jumped back, startled, but then he realized that the man was still alive, not merely twitching. He knelt down beside him, but he had no idea where to begin repairing the man's ruined body. He had no medicine, hypo, first aid kit, nothing but dirty hands and a disruptor pistol.

"Try to relax," Geordi told the dying man. "Help is on the way."

Blue Moon fumbled for Geordi's arm, and gripping it, he did seem to relax. But his breathing was horribly labored, and he bled from wounds that Geordi couldn't even see.

Hoarsely, Blue Moon said, "Tell them—tell them we died bravely. Killing Cardassians."

"Who should I tell?" asked Geordi.

"Tell any ship going into the DMZ." Blue Moon

coughed up blood, and he drew a breath that sounded like a broken bellows.

"What's your real name?" asked Geordi. "And the names of the others?"

The young man wheezed as if trying to get enough breath to finish. "Just tell them . . . crew of the *Shufola*. They know us. . . ."

His voice trailed off, and his eyes shut halfway. Geordi felt the man's grip loosen on his arm, then his hand fell away. Although he knew it was useless, he felt for a pulse, but the man called Blue Moon had joined his fellow Maquis on the next plain of existence.

Geordi yanked the Bajoran comm badge off the officer's chest and pushed his eyes shut before he stood up. He squinted through his VISOR at the pockmarked beach, hoping that rain and high tides would heal it in time. He couldn't speed that process, but he could do something about the corpses and the spent weapons.

The engineer drew his disruptor, pointed it at Blue Moon, and ran the fiery beam along his body until there was nothing left but a few ashes. One by one, he disposed of the bodies of the Maquis officers, wishing he could leave some sort of gravestone for them, a marker that stated they had died in battle on a very foreign shore. He couldn't do that, but he vowed to relay Blue Moon's message to the first Maquis ship he encountered, so that someone might remember them.

When the bodies were gone, Geordi lifted the Bajoran comm badge to his ear and pressed it. As far as he knew, there were no ships in orbit except for the Cardassian vessel, but he couldn't stay on this planet a moment longer. They had made enough of a mess, and now it was time to vacate. Commander Riker and Admiral Nechayev had died trying to uphold the Prime Directive, and at least Geordi could leave when everyone else did.

He squeezed the comm badge again, hoping the Cardassians were monitoring the frequency. "This is Lieutenant Commander Geordi La Forge of the starship *Enterprise*. Please come in. This is La Forge on the planet's surface, please come in."

"Mr. La Forge!" came a startled but pleased voice. "This is Captain Picard, and I'm very relieved to hear your voice."

"Captain!" Geordi grinned. "This is a big relief for me, too. We walked away from the landing, sort of, but that saucer is never going to fly again."

"We know," answered the captain. "We've readied a photon torpedo to sink it for good. You'll be happy to know that we have rescued Commander Riker and Admiral Nechayev."

"Thank God!" Geordi whispered. "I guess once you get me we're done here."

"So we didn't suffer any personnel losses?"

Geordi blinked thoughtfully into the sun. "No, all the dead were Maquis, and some Cardassians. They killed each other."

"Any reason to go after the Cardassian vessel? We could catch them."

Geordi thought about the sniveling traitor who had caused so much death and destruction. Was there a punishment to fit the crime? Probably not under Federation statutes.

"The Cardassians did capture one Maquis," he finally answered. "But I doubt if he'll live long enough to be rescued. I don't think it's worth going to war over."

"Then we'll let it end here." stated Picard.

The engineer nodded wearily. Picard did not wait for his reply.

"Stand by to beam up. Do you require medical attention?"

Geordi considered the grime packed on every centimeter of his body. "No, sir, just a shower."

In the cargo hold of the Cardassian warship *Taranor,* Gul Awarkin leaned over the scrawny, naked body of Henry Fulton, which was bound tightly and stretched across an antimatter storage pod. He ran the handle of his Ferengi plasma whip down Fulton's spine, increasing the human's pathetic whimpering.

"You are the one code-named Peacock, are you not?" asked the Gul.

"I'm a Starfleet officer, a double agent!" shouted Fulton. "Let me go, I demand it."

"Are you Peacock?" The Gul uncurled the whip and lashed the slender threads across the back of Fulton's thighs. He shrieked in pain as sparks of plasma scorched his flesh.

"Yes! Yes!" he screamed. "I'm Peacock! I'm Peacock! Aaaagh!"

"Good," said the Cardassian, well pleased. "I see this Ferengi whip is as efficient as advertised, at least on humans. I picked it up on a recent visit to Deep Space Nine from a very amusing fellow.

Now, we have established *you* are Peacock. Who is Blue Moon?"

Fulton started blubbering. "I don't know! I mean, you *killed* him!"

"But we still need to know who he is—to see if he had any family or friends who might also be causing trouble in the Demilitarized Zone. What was his name?"

When Fulton only stared, the Gul flicked the tendrils of the Ferengi whip upon his backside, and the man's wretched howl was so loud that it reverberated in the cargo hold.

"I don't know!" he groaned.

"I doubt that," said the Gul. "But if you will tell me one thing, I promise to let you go, unharmed."

"Yes, yes!"

"Who is the Architect?"

"I don't know!"

"You'll tell me who the Architect is, or this trip could be very unpleasant." The Cardassian raked the sparkling whip across the entire length of Fulton's body, and his screams sounded loud enough to carry through the titanium walls of the craft and into space.

When Captain Picard reached sickbay, Will Riker was already sitting up in bed. A padd rested in his lap on top of the blanket, as if he had been making a few notes.

When Riker seemed about to rise, the captain gestured for him to relax. "At ease, Will."

The commander smiled. "I take it things have calmed down."

The captain nodded in agreement. "We were lucky to get out of it with as little damage as we did. That was a commendable job under very trying circumstances."

"You too, sir." Both men glanced in the direction of Admiral Nechayev, who was also sitting up in her bed at the far end of the room. Dr. Crusher was chatting with her.

Picard cleared his throat. "At least we won't have to explain this one to the admiral."

"No," said Riker, "but we may have a hard time explaining it to anyone else." He gazed at the admiral briefly. "She's an extraordinary woman. You should have heard the tongue-lashings she gave those Maquis, even after they used her for a punching bag."

"I'm sure," said Picard with a pained smile. "It's not everyone who can order her own death. That gave me a turn, I can tell you. So, even though we're shorthanded, are you being taken care of?"

At that moment, Deanna Troi and Guinan came marching through the door, carrying trays of food. Riker smiled at the captain. "I'm okay."

Picard patted his first officer on the back and continued to the opposite end of the room. At his approach, the admiral and the doctor halted their conversation and smiled at him.

The captain bowed stiffly. "Admiral Nechayev, I'm glad to see you're looking so well."

"I look like hell, Captain," she answered hoarsely, "but considering the alternative, that's all right with me."

At the same time, they both said, "I'm sorry. . . ."

The captain looked down, embarrassed, but the admiral appeared angry as she replied, "*You* can't take any blame for this fiasco, it was *my* doing. I brought the snake into the nest, and my report on your conduct and that of your officers will contain nothing but the highest praise. In particular, Riker and La Forge. No wonder you'll do anything to hold on to them."

Nechayev leaned back, looking weary, and Beverly Crusher hovered a bit closer to the battered woman.

"I'll behave myself," she told the doctor. "The captain is only staying another minute. You know, Captain, I travel on starships all the time, but I never belong to them, never feel part of the crew. Riker and La Forge made me feel a part of your crew, and for that experience I am grateful."

She scowled and crossed her arms. "But I could do without some of the rest of it. After this experience, I intend to revise my opinion about landing a saucer on a planet. I'm not going to suggest it anymore, except under dire circumstances, which I presume a captain will recognize when he encounters them."

"I doubt if it will ever happen," said Picard with a reassuring smile. "And as for the prototype, we have a torpedo ready to sink it. It's only a matter of time before it goes under, but Data thinks the Pedrians have canoes. So we would prefer to hurry it along."

"Go ahead and sink it." The admiral shivered and pulled the blanket tighter around her shoulders. "The native people are not going deep into that seawater, I can tell you."

"Data estimates that it will be two millennia before the Pedrians develop the technology needed to find the wreck. And La Forge made sure there was nothing left on land."

"Where is Henry Fulton?" asked the admiral with distaste.

"As far as we know, he perished with the other Maquis in a battle with Cardassians."

The admiral shook her head as if she had absorbed enough insanity for one day. "Cardassians," she muttered. "For them, we've turned our own people into ruthless murderers. There must be another way, a way to bring the Maquis back into the Federation."

Picard sighed. "Not while they let hatred guide their actions."

Nechayev nodded slowly and closed her eyes. "I believe the doctor would like me to rest now, Captain. And you should rest, too. I'm adding three days of shore leave to the *Enterprise*'s schedule."

Beverly smiled at Picard, and he nodded absently at her, still preoccupied with the job at hand. "Thank you, sir. All right, let's finish our mission." He tapped his comm badge. "Picard to bridge. Launch torpedo and destroy target."

"Yes, sir," answered Commander Data. "Lieutenant Worf, you may fire when ready."

On the choppy turquoise ocean of Pedrum, the

gleaming new island floated sluggishly, only a few pockets of air keeping it buoyant. Black clouds curled across the sky, waiting to return more water to the mineral-rich sea. Had a Pedrian been watching this scene, he would have sworn that the heavens opened up and a bolt of lightning streaked down ripping into the center of the saucer, shooting a column of seawater a kilometer into the air. The immense disc cracked into dozens of pieces, like a badly cut pie, and the pieces slipped into the churning sea as bubbles erupted all across the surface.

Several birds swooped over the bubbles, squawking urgently, but they couldn't prevent the shattered saucer from slipping into the cold depths. With a final, cockeyed spurt of water, the ship glided beneath the agitated waves, not to be seen again by air-breathing creatures for millennia.

Chapter Sixteen

THE SLIM BAJORAN WOMAN sat on a bluff overlooking the Kylatir Meadows, which had been strip-mined and deserted by the Cardassians over thirty years earlier. The meadows were only now returning to their natural state of lush grasslands, wildflowers, and muddy streams. Here and there were mounds of quarried rocks, looking like unhealed scabs upon the land.

Behind her in the camp she heard the voices of her fellow Maquis, about half Bajoran and half human in number, all of them dispossessed of land by the Cardassians. They were talking about her again, angry that the almighty Architect had made them camp out on Bajor for a week while no one but the Prophets knew what was happening in the

DMZ. Worse yet, she had allowed none of them to visit family and friends, although all of them longed to do so.

Yes, the Architect had to admit, she was hiding out. She was enjoying a brief respite from the killing and the planning of killing to watch the wildflowers blossom in a meadow. So to hell with them. The Maquis had wanted her, not the other way around. Starfleet had pushed her into their arms, and they had grabbed ahold—but she was still her own woman. While most of them had been forced into this violent existence after their homes had been seized, the Architect had joined of her own free will. She had given up her former life and her modest possessions for *them,* and they should damn well remember it.

She tossed a stone on the ground and watched it roll into the basin. This remote area, where they had landed the shuttlecraft and camped, was known to be a resistance stronghold in the old days when the Cardassians had occupied Bajor. The locals left food and clothing for them, but they gave them a wide berth, knowing instinctively that they were still in the fight. They had that haunted, twitchy look about them, she supposed, the look of people who were on a first-name basis with death.

The Architect had waited here a week, hoping to hear something on the grapevine—about a Galaxy-class starship being hijacked from Starfleet. Such news would reach them even here, but they hadn't heard a peep. She gazed at the peaceful meadow for a few more minutes, thinking that she couldn't delay the inevitable. They had to go back, or the entire movement would be demoralized. She stood up, brushed the fresh pollen off her pants, and strode back to the clearing.

A couple of the Maquis were striking the tents and loading the shuttlecraft, but the other dozen or so were just staring sullenly at her as she approached. Some still thought it was her fault that they had been rooted out of New Hope and driven here, with crucial files falling into enemy hands. If they wanted to feel that way, it was fine with her. In reality, it *was* her fault, because the actions of their cell had been uncommonly successful, scaring the hell out of the Cardassians. The fact that the Cardassians had come after her with a veritable army only proved it. She would be ready for that tactic next time.

The Architect could have shared these innermost thoughts with her comrades, but she was tired of giving them pep talks. She pointed to the underbelly of their battered shuttlecraft and said, "I thought I told you to take those phaser emitters off."

"Aw, come on," growled one of the human males. "Why should we throw away perfectly good phasers and leave ourselves unarmed?" There was muttered agreement from a few of the others.

The Bajoran put her hands on her hips and glared at him. "Why? Because we want to get back to the DMZ without being captured. At least *I* don't want to be captured. Maybe the rest of you are ready to give up."

The man took a threatening step toward her.

"You can't say that about us. We were doing fine *before* you came."

"Then leave me here." The Architect stared defiantly at him. "I'll live off roots and berries and be better off than I am with you people. But if you want me to go back with you, you'll take the damn phasers off the shuttlecraft right now!"

Then she grabbed an empty toolbox and tossed it clattering to the ground. "And throw your disruptor pistols into this box, so we can collect them and bury them!"

When no one moved to end or further the mutiny, the blond woman stepped hesitantly forward. Her eyes were still red from crying over the husband she had left behind on New Hope. "The Architect is right," she told them. "If we're going to get past Starfleet's blockade, we can't have a single weapon on our ship. We've got to look like civilians."

She unstrapped her holster and tossed the disruptor pistol into the metal box. Reluctantly, the others did the same, even the human who had challenged the Architect.

"That's better," said their leader in a conciliatory tone. "I don't like this either, but we can't do any good rotting away in a Federation prison. Besides, we know Starfleet is in a very grouchy mood after the freighter faked them out two weeks ago."

A few of the Maquis chuckled, and several of them went to the shuttlecraft and started to unbolt the phasers from the underbelly of the craft. The

Architect sighed and let her taut shoulders relax, wondering if there was any way to leave the Maquis, other than to join the Prophets.

The next day, the Maquis shuttlecraft was approaching the demilitarized zone at warp one, and the Architect was leaning over the shoulder of her pilot, a Bajoran woman even younger than herself. Both of them were watching a large blip on their short-range sensors, wondering if it would reach them before they reached the DMZ.

"They've increased speed," said the pilot. "They're definitely on a course to intercept."

"They're hailing us," reported the copilot, pressing her headphone against her ear. Her eyes widened with shock. "They identify themselves as the *Enterprise!*"

The Architect winced, knowing that if the *Enterprise* was here, the mission had probably failed.

"Just remain calm," she told the two women in the cockpit. "I'm going to scrunch down under the instrument panel and stay out of sight while you answer their hail—on screen. Remember, we're civilians coming back from a visit to Bajor for Feast Days."

The Architect got on her hands and knees and crawled under the lip of the copilot's console, where she could observe everything but not be seen by the visual recorder. The rest of their band was safely ensconced in the passenger section with orders not to come into the cockpit under any circumstances. Crouched out of sight, the Architect nodded to her pilot, who punched up the scowling, bearded face of Commander Will Riker on the small viewscreen.

"This is civilian transport Qoaka coming back from Bajor," the pilot announced.

"You're not carrying any weapons, are you?"

"No, sir," the Bajoran answered brightly, "just celebrants for the Feast Days."

Riker sounded doubtful or maybe just weary as he replied, "By the terms of our agreement with the Cardassians, there are contraband weapons that are not allowed in the DMZ. Please come to a full stop, lower your shields, and prepare to be scanned. It will take only a moment."

"We understand," said the pilot with an honest sigh of relief.

After a nod from the Architect, the pilot brought the shuttlecraft out of warp drive and to a complete stop. Like an avenging Goliath come to smite David, the starship *Enterprise* cruised into the path of the tiny vessel and came to a stop. The Architect could imagine Data efficiently scanning the shuttlecraft and reporting the negative results.

The handsome commander finally granted the pilot a smile. "I see you carry no weaponry. We're sorry for the delay."

"Think nothing of it," answered the woman. The Architect could see the woman's leg trembling.

"Uh, there's just one thing." added Riker, "My chief engineer would like to speak with you for a moment."

As the commander stepped aside, the Architect glanced at her pilot and shook her head. She couldn't fathom why Geordi La Forge would want to speak with them, unless it was to warn about some equipment problem they had spotted during the scan. The pilot kept her pleasant smile plastered to her face while her leg shook like a reed in a hurricane.

A man with a gentle face and a VISOR appeared on the screen and bowed somewhat apologetically. "If you're going to the DMZ, would you relay a message?"

The pilot nodded eagerly. "Certainly. To whom?"

"I don't know exactly," answered Geordi with a shrug. "I don't mean to insinuate that you are involved with the Maquis, but this message is for any Maquis sympathizers you might know or run across."

The Architect held her breath and bit her lip. She had a terrible premonition of what was coming next.

"The freighter *Shufola*," he began, "was destroyed in action. All hands are dead."

The copilot gasped, and the pilot kept smiling stiffly, although her leg stopped twitching and held as still as a tree trunk. Luckily, the Architect was crouched out of sight, so she didn't wipe away the salty tear that rolled down her gaunt cheek and onto her lip.

"Several of them died fighting Cardassians," said Geordi. "They wanted someone to remember them, and this is the best we can do under the circumstances."

"All right," rasped the pilot, "I'll pass the word if

I encounter anyone who's interested. Can we go now?"

"Certainly," said the Engineer. "Sorry for the inconvenience. *Enterprise* out."

The screen returned to a wide view of the starscape and the massive flagship of the Federation. With a sudden burst of light, the *Enterprise* went into reverse and vanished like a retreating headlight into the distance. The pilot pounded her fist on the console, and the copilot covered her eyes and wept.

The Architect rose wearily to her feet, feeling as if she had aged into an old widow. She pushed back her short-cropped hair and stared out the window of the shuttlecraft at a sparkling vista of stars suspended in infinity. It looked no different than any other sector of space, except for the fact that good men and women were willing to die for it.